The Forgotten Knight

Emilie DeRitter

outskirtspress
DENVER, COLORADO

The Forgotten Knight

v6.0

Illustrated by: Lisa Griffin

Outskirts Press, Inc.
http://www.outskirtspress.com

ISBN: 978-1-4327-9800-0

PRINTED IN THE UNITED STATES OF AMERICA

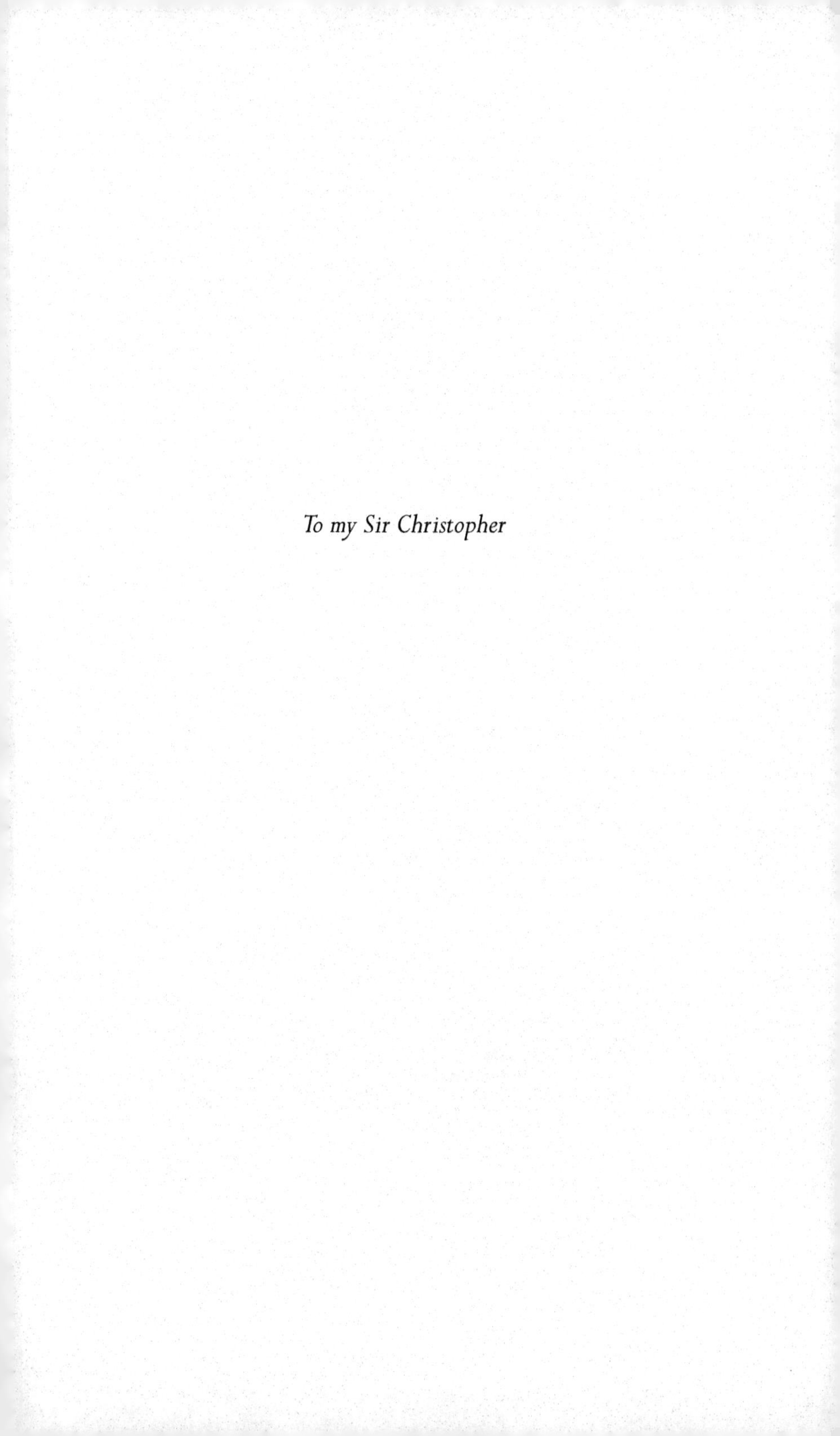

To my Sir Christopher

contents

acknowledgements

There are so many people that helped with this book, it's hard to know where to begin. First, thank you to Christopher, for without him I would have had no idea. Thank you to Nicole for her typing skills and for lending a certain princess her personality. Thank you to Kevin and Robert, who asked all the right questions. To Lydia, Tawnya, and Dr. Ledbetter for helping me create such vivid secondary characters. To Mikey and Mama Carole, for without you the process of rewriting would have been unbearable.

To Mom and Dad, the devoted believer and the converted skeptic.

To the students of Almondale Jr. High – your opinions mattered.

And lastly, thank you to Rae, for without her this entire project would still be unfinished, gathering dust in some long forgotten corner of my mind. Thank you, my friend, for being the die-hard believer and the driving force behind me, no matter what.

Chapter I
A Cry for Help

"Help!" The stillness of the forest was broken by a sharp feminine cry. Startled by the shrillness of it, a lone traveler on a large chestnut warhorse turned in his saddle, his helm glinting in the sun as he moved. His dark, penetrating eyes scanned the trees through his raised visor. Having come to a decision about the best direction to proceed, he squeezed his armor-clad knees into the horse's sides and galloped off into the forest.

Perched in a nearby tree, a larger than average red-tailed hawk watched as Sir Christopher of Calidore took off on his next adventure. "Here we go again," she muttered as she flapped her wings and took to the skies to follow the valiant hero. Several moments later, she spotted Sir Christopher's horse, Jonathan, waiting patiently for the hero's return. The hawk turned her head in every direction before she demanded aloud, "Chris! Where are you?"

His voice filtered down through the leaves of one of the taller trees in the area. "I'm trying to get a lay of the land."

She landed on the top most branch of the tree, a stone's throw above the knight. "You don't look like you can see a whole lot from where you are."

He glanced up at her. "If you think this is easy, maybe next time I can fly and you can climb the tree wearing full armor. Now be quiet. I need to concentrate."

The hawk snapped her beak in frustration. While waiting for Christopher to continue climbing, she turned her head from side to side, surveying the landscape. "So … what are we doing up here?" she asked.

He fumbled around as the branch he had tried to use as a handhold snapped under his weight. He glared at her. "The plan was to get up to where you are so that I could determine where the call for help is coming from."

"Well, you can stop climbing then because you won't be able to see anything other than forest once you get up here."

He sighed in frustration. "For someone of supposedly unmatched intelligence, you certainly are dense. You're a hawk. Flap your wings and get a bird's eye view of everything while I figure out how to get down."

"Well, I like that. How did I get stuck doing all the work around here?"

"Aurora, please. Just do me this favor."

"Oh, fine. Have it your way." With that, she took off and soared high above the treetops, circling Christopher's position while gradually widening her search. She finally noticed a small, secluded castle nestled deep in the forest. As she flew nearer, the cries for help grew louder, but the louder they got, the less urgent they sounded. She quickly flew back to Christopher, who by that time had managed to get both feet back on the ground.

"Well, I found her, but you aren't going to like this. She doesn't sound distressed, just shrill and bored. She's in a castle, hidden in the forest, nearly half a league from here."

"Bored, huh?"

"Don't forget shrill."

"Well, you know as well as I do that we cannot ignore a call for help. So, bored or not, we go."

The bird scoffed. "It's going to be a long day."

The horse stamped his hoof impatiently. "Alright, boy, we're going." The horse knelt down so that Sir Christopher could easily mount the saddle in his armor, and then they galloped through the forest toward the castle.

When they reached the edge of the small clearing that surrounded the castle, Christopher removed his helm. His dark curly hair fell down, nearly covering his eyes. "This is not good." His youthful face had a pensive look on it.

Aurora perched on a low hanging tree branch nearby and also surveyed the situation. The castle was surrounded by a ten-foot wide moat and the drawbridge was up. There was a thin strip of land on the other side of the moat, and the stones were worn enough that there appeared to be a decent amount of handholds all the way up the wall. "I hate to be the bearer of bad news, but I can only come up with two ways to get in."

"And are you able to do one of them?" he asked as he began removing his armor.

"Uh … no … not actually."

"Then it looks like I'm going to get wet." The heavy metal armor made plenty of noise as he dropped it, piece by piece, in a pile by Jonathan's forelegs. Without his armor, he was of average height and build, perhaps even undersized for a knight. His face was young, betraying his age as early twenties. He ran his hand over his slightly stubbly chin as he stared at the moat.

Aurora swooped down and tested the water with her wing. "I wonder why the moat is just water."

"Is there anything dangerous in the moat?" he asked as he prepared to jump in.

"Define dangerous."

"You're no help, you know that!"

She scoffed. "Not that I could see."

"Did you even look?" he grumbled, sitting down, his feet in the water.

"I resent that remark!" the hawk sputtered indignantly.

"Yeah, well, history has a tendency to repeat itself when you're around. Are you going to do your job this time?"

"I always do my job," she grumbled. Then, as an afterthought, "Be careful."

He slid into the murky water, with only his sword and dagger for his protection, and flashed her his charismatic grin. "This is what I live for!"

"Don't I know it."

He managed to swim about halfway across the moat before a feeling of dread crept into the pit of his stomach. "Are you sure there's nothing dangerous in here?" he asked, turning back in her direction. As he did so, he found himself face to face with a gaping mouth full of teeth. "Aurora!" he screamed in panic as the creature tried to take a bite out of him and missed. "Do something!" He managed to drop his sword into the depths of the murky water.

"That explains a few things." With a puff of smoke, the hawk was replaced with a young woman crouched by the water's edge. She was tall, nearly as tall as Christopher, with a long, lithe body dressed in black leggings and a deep green tunic. Her long, brilliant blood red hair was tied back in a loose ponytail, falling in waves to her waist. Her narrow face was set with determination but her green eyes glowed with mischief when she moved her hand as if to cast a spell. However, he didn't see his situation improve.

He muttered something about feminine moodiness as he struggled to situate himself on its back. "What in blazes is this thing?" he yelled, managing to wrap his arms around its jaws to keep it from snapping up one of his appendages.

"It's a crocodile," she replied, sounding as if they were describing a tapestry on a wall rather than his current adversary. "It's a rather aggressive reptile, distant relative of the dinosaurs, native to the continents … oops!" She clasped both hands firmly over her open mouth when she realized that she was revealing the future.

"Crocodile? Dinosaur?" He had by this time resorted to unsheathing his dagger and using it in an attempt to penetrate the creature's tough hide. "You do realize I have no idea what you're talking about?"

"Sorry! Are you okay?"

"Fine … no thanks to you," he grumbled, still struggling with the large creature.

"Sometimes, I think you have no appreciation for all I do for you."

"Please, focus!"

With a splash of water and a thrashing of bodies, he found himself alone in the water, and the creature had vanished from view. He had also now managed to drop his knife into the murky water as well. "Where is it? Can you see it?" he asked, frantically swimming back in the direction he had come from. "Were you planning to do your job at some point?!"

"I'm sorry … were you asking for my help?"

"If I live through this…!" he bellowed as the creature wrapped its jaws around his midsection and began to bite down.

With a snap of her fingers, they were both high and dry inside the walls of the castle.

"Why didn't you turn him into a guppy when this whole mess started?" he demanded, shaking his head to remove water from his ear.

She smiled. "Too easy. Answer me this: Are you cut?"

"What? What do you mean?"

"Are you bleeding? Are you injured?"

He looked down at his midsection and all his limbs. To his amazement, only his clothes showed evidence that he'd been in a fight with the creature. "Uh … no."

"Precisely." With that, she drew her own knife from its sheath, grabbed his forearm and thrust the knife into his bare skin. Upon coming in contact with him, the knife blade crumpled as if made of paper. "The spell will wear off in about an hour. Next time, just ***trust*** me."

"You make it so difficult sometimes." He shook his head and began walking forward, secretly smiling to himself about the craftiness of his partner.

Chapter II
The Tower Prisoner

They cautiously walked through the castle, following the very bored cries for help.

"Help. Please, someone, help me. I could really use some help."

"Maybe we should just kill her and put her out of her misery," Aurora joked, earning a glare of disapproval from the knight.

"That wasn't funny," he scolded.

She shrugged her shoulders and continued grinning, her slightly malicious humor having been lost on her good-hearted companion.

They found themselves standing at the base of the tower, staring up the stairs. Christopher silently thanked his moody guardian angel for retrieving his sword and dagger when she'd plucked him from death's jaws. He took a deep breath.

"I know, I know," she muttered, quickly transforming into a large black jaguar, "Watch your back."

He smiled. "Ready?"

She swished her tail twice in acknowledgement and he started up the stairs, the cat close on his heels. The stairs wound around the tower and ended at a locked wooden door. He drew his sword and glanced back at his guardian. With a nod from her, he shouldered the door open with a loud bang and dropped to his knees, the jaguar leaping over him, much to the surprise of the room's sole occupant.

"Careful!" the no longer bored voice screamed. "If you break the mirror I am done for!"

The cat skidded to a halt and Christopher looked up in surprise to see a shimmering reflection in a large mirror that was not his own. Aurora circled the mirror in a predatory fashion. "This is definitely unexpected." She looked up at him. "Any ideas?"

He looked at the mirror again and it registered that the reflection was that of a young princess. She was a head shorter than he was and she was dressed in a silver gown that sparkled in the sunlight coming through the window, her blonde hair piled on the top of her head with curls cascading down. She peered back at him wide-eyed through her glass prison.

"Are you a knight?" she asked in disbelief.

Dusting himself off and climbing to his feet, he looked up in surprise. "Yes, I am."

"Then where is your armor?" she asked suspiciously.

He glanced down, slightly caught off guard because he wasn't wearing it. "I took it off."

"Why would you do a thing like that?"

"I had to swim the moat."

Her bright blue eyes narrowed suspiciously. "You do not appear wet."

"I vote we leave her in there," Aurora said haughtily.

"Aurora!" he warned.

"Fine. Then can I eat her?"

He smiled. "I wouldn't suggest it. You know I hate it when you have indigestion, it makes the journey so much more difficult."

"Excuse me, but ***I*** do not find your idle prattle amusing," the princess stated flatly, adopting a lofty tone.

He politely attempted to hide a grin as he turned to Aurora. "Can you get her out?"

She shook her feline head. "I already thought of that. The spell that's holding her as a reflection has some serious power behind it."

The bored princess sighed in frustration. "So, how do a tattered boy pretending to be a knight and a talking pussycat plan to rescue me from this wizard if a dozen ***real*** knights that have come before you have failed?"

"Tattered ***boy***?" Christopher exclaimed, examining his ragged clothes that usually went between the padding for his armor and his skin.

"***Pussycat***?" Aurora demanded.

"***Pretending*** to be a knight?"

"***Now*** can I eat her?"

Before he could answer, a tenuous tune floated through the open door, announcing the approach of the wizard responsible for the unlikely situation they found themselves in.

"Here comes trouble," Christopher muttered, brandishing his sword and backing up until his back was nearly touching the surface of the mirror. Aurora's tail swished in anticipation as a short, grizzled old wizard entered the room, whistling obliviously.

"Well, my little turtledove, have you given any more thought to my…" his voice trailed off at the sight of the unorthodox intruders and his black eyes narrowed. "I did not realize that your mother had run out of knights already. Like a squire is going to fare any better!"

"Squire?!" Christopher sputtered.

"Now you've done it," Aurora laughed. "He's very sensitive about his appearance today."

The old wizard stared at the jaguar in confusion. He reached up to run his right hand through the grizzled mop of hair on his head, causing his blue and grey robes to rustle and reveal a green talisman dangling from his neck just below his beard. "That voice … it's … I know that voice."

"My good sir, if you truly believe yourself to be a knight, then rescue me from this fiend!"

Christopher threw up his free hand in frustration. "Aurora, any ideas?"

The jaguar crouched into a pouncing position as a devilish grin crossed her face. "Just one."

"Aurora … of Beldain?" the wizard gaped in recognition, his hand flying to his chest just as she leapt through the air, pinning him flat on his back on the floor under her massive paws, his fingers only inches away from the talisman.

"I'll take that," she said, grasping the talisman in her teeth and yanking it from his neck.

"You foolish woman!" he screeched at Aurora. "You have no idea what you'll unleash!"

Christopher raised his eyebrows in confusion, but before he could ask what the wizard was referring to, he vanished from beneath Aurora's paws in a rather pathetic puff of smoke.

"Varuk is getting rather cryptic in his old age," Aurora said, transforming into human form and holding the talisman in her left hand.

"You *did* know him?" Christopher asked cautiously.

"Yes. And that was a little too easy, even for him." Her hair shimmered to a copper color in annoyance as if to match her change in temperament.

He sighed. "I was afraid of that."

Aurora knelt down to examine the engravings on the mirror's frame. As she ran her hand along the elaborate carvings, she sucked in a sharp breath. "Chris, you're not gonna like this!" She looked up and noticed that he was down on one knee in the middle of the floor, his left hand clasped around the hilt of his sword, his right clutching the gold cross that hung from his neck, and his head bowed in prayer. "And, of course, you're busy."

It was only at that moment that she realized that the exceptionally vocal princess had been uncharacteristically silent. She looked up to find the princess, mouth agape, glancing back and forth between the two travelers. "Cat got your tongue?" she asked with a devious glint in her eye.

"You are a witch!"

Aurora sputtered in indignation, her hair color flaring from blood colored to scarlet. "I beg your pardon?!" She spun around to Christopher. "I'm not helping! I'm leaving her in there!"

"Good sir, do protect me from your … what *is* he doing?!"

"Problem solving. When he doesn't know how to proceed, he asks for divine intervention … or something like that."

"You are a witch. Can you not just wave your magic wand and get me out?"

"First of all: you're mixing stereotypes. Second: I am not some human with limited magical skills; I am a ***sorceress***, a magical being. Big difference! Witch indeed! Third: I can't use my magic to do it for him!"

"A sorceress who cannot use magic? How useless!"

"Yeah, we'll see how useless I am when I turn you into a toad!"

"You would not dare! I am of noble blood!"

"It's so cute how you think that matters. When he's done, I'm gonna let him get you out ... without my help."

"You mean to say that you are unable to do anything besides stand there helplessly waiting for him."

Aurora let out a forced breath of frustration. "Conniving little...!" she muttered as she pulled a pinch of blue powder from a pouch on her belt and sprinkled it on the surface of the glass. There was a bright flash and a thunderous boom, causing the princess to shut her eyes and cover both ears. When she dared to peek, she saw Christopher kneeling beside his companion, fumbling with a small bag of powder he had pulled from her belt.

"Stubborn...! Just had to prove your point...! Let her bait you...! You never learn!" His calloused fingers had finally managed to undo the delicate knot on the pouch, revealing a fine grained black powder. He sprinkled a small amount of the powder on Aurora and she began to shrink and change form until she had become a ferret that he draped gently across his shoulders.

"One good thing came out of this," Aurora whispered. "It showed me what to do. The talisman is the key." She groaned softly. "Somewhere in the frame."

"And now to deal with you, Milady," he said, picking up the discarded talisman and his sword as he slowly got to his feet, trying not to jostle the injured Aurora.

"Good sir! I beg you! Do not use your magic on me!"

He sighed in frustration, sheathed his sword and began to examine the frame of the mirror. He placed his now empty right hand on the frame and slid it down until he found a recess that was about the same size as the talisman. He peered around the side, slid the talisman into the hole and watched as the surface of the mirror shimmered and moved like water. "Your hand, Milady," he commanded, holding his hand out to help her step down.

Her eyes went wide as she cautiously reached out her hand for his. To her utter amazement, her hand passed right through the glass as if it were the surface of a pond. He firmly grasped her hand and helped her through the mirror.

As soon as she had both feet firmly on the ground, she unceremoniously retracted her hand from his, proclaiming "You, ***sir***, are no knight!"

He sighed and reached his hand around the back of the mirror, deftly removing the talisman from its notch. As he did so, the frame immediately crumbled to dust. "Milady, it has been a long day and my companion needs rest. So, if there is nothing more I can do for you, Lady…"

"Gwenyth. Princess Gwenyth of Aliwyn." She drew herself up to her full height and was still a head shorter than he was.

"Well, Princess Gwenyth of Aliwyn, I bid you farewell."

The princess' mouth fell open in horror. "You simply ***cannot*** leave me here alone! What if Varuk comes back?! He will come up with something else horrible to do to force me to marry him!"

He smiled as he started down the stairs. "Why are you asking me? I thought protecting damsels in distress was a job for a ***real*** knight?"

She picked up her skirt and scurried after him. "I take it back. I believe you! You ***are*** a knight!"

"You should have left her in the mirror," Aurora said faintly. Christopher only smiled.

Chapter III
A Tale of Friendship

"Ugh, my good sir, I refuse to walk one step further!"
He let out a small sigh as he pulled the lever that would lower the drawbridge. "Milady, if you would be willing to walk a mere thirty paces more, we will reach my horse, my armor, and a clearing where we may spend the night."

"So close to the castle? What if Varuk returns?"

"He won't," Aurora whispered. "We're safe … for tonight."

Christopher smiled at the princess with reassurance. "Aurora assures me that Varuk will not return tonight. We shall be safe here until the morrow."

The princess rolled her eyes. "Then why not spend the night in the castle?" she demanded. "There are beds enough for all of us." She gestured toward the stone walls that had held her captive just as they evanesced. "Goodness!" she shrieked, running to catch up with Christopher so that she could drape her arm through his and be protected from any other strange occurrences that might arise. "I never did thank you for rescuing me."

"You still haven't," he said with a smile.

She suppressed a sigh of frustration. "Thank you for rescuing me, Sir…"

"Christopher … of Calidore," he finished for her.

"From the legends? The fabled traveler who helps those in need? The cursed knight whom Providence forgot?"

"Sir Christopher will be just fine, thank you."

A confused look crossed her regal features at the knight's reaction to the reference to his legends, but, by this time, they had reached the clearing where Jonathan had been patiently grazing and waiting for their return. The petite princess glanced up at the large war horse with apprehension since he was nearly as tall as Christopher at the shoulder and barrel-chested. "Is he dangerous?"

Christopher shook his head. "Only in battle. The rest of the time he's perfectly amiable." He pulled a blanket roll from Jonathan's saddle and began unrolling it on the ground. "He likes it if you pet his nose."

Gwenyth warily reached her hand up, prompting the horse to bend his neck so she could stroke the velveteen nose. "What is his name?"

"Jonathan."

"That seems a funny name for a war horse. Why Jonathan? Why not something grander?"

He lowered his eyebrows in confusion, as if she'd just asked him a trick question. "He's named after King David's best friend, Jonathan, the son of King Saul. It was the best and most true example of friendship in the Bible."

She knitted her brows and just stared at him for a moment before shrugging it off and turning her attention back to the horse. "I still think it is a funny name." With that she reached her hand forward to pet his nose again, but Jonathan snorted in ire and jerked his head up beyond her reach. Her mouth fell open slightly at this vexation, but then she turned her attention to Christopher and Aurora the ferret. "So, what is your story exactly?"

He looked up from the firewood he had gathered into a pile. "What do you mean?"

"I have heard the stories and they cannot possibly be true."

"What do these 'stories' say?" He struck his knife against his flint, causing sparks.

"They tell your story to young princes and knights as a cautionary tale. They say that your story is what happens when your curiosity and ambition drive you instead of honor, duty and … chivalry. They say that you cut the horn from a unicorn because you wanted its magic and you are being punished. You are forced to do good deeds until the end of your days to make amends."

He chuckled in annoyance. "That story has definitely changed in form over time."

"Then you did not cut the horn from a unicorn?"

"No," he said, gently placing Aurora on a corner of the bedroll so that she could curl up and go to sleep. "I wouldn't dare lay a hand on a unicorn. I respect their magic too much."

"Then perhaps you would care to enlighten me as to what really did happen?"

He laughed and shook his head. "All right, I will tell you what really happened if you tell me why you were so convinced that I wasn't a knight."

She glanced around and finally decided to sit on the bedroll, her skirt billowing out around her as she did so. "Agreed." She pushed her nose into the air to regain her dignity. "The missing armor and the torn clothes were definitely not confidence inspiring. But to be perfectly honest, your hands were what had me convinced."

He narrowed his eyes and looked down at his calloused hands. "Why?"

She snickered. "I do not care how much sparring you do or how many wars you fight in, the hands of a true knight would never get as calloused as those of a farmer."

"Carpenter, actually."

"What?"

"Before I was a knight, I was a carpenter. Well, an apprentice anyway."

"A carpenter's apprentice? Varuk was bested by a carpenter's apprentice?"

"You never know what you can do until you try," he said with a shrug.

"Now I have to hear the whole story."

He smiled and sat down with his back against a tree. The flames crackled and their glow reflected in his dark eyes as they took on a far-away look. "I was born in the province of Calidore, the eldest son of a poor farmer. When I was seven, I was apprenticed to a carpenter in another town. At the age of fifteen, my apprenticeship was transferred to the kingdom's ruler when the carpenter passed, and he chose to pass it to his younger son. However, the son was a knight in the court of King Lionel and had no use for an apprentice, so I became his squire. I won't bore you with tales of my time as a squire, but by the time I was eighteen, I was a knight. King Lionel knighted me to thank me for rescuing his daughter from a dragon.

"After I was knighted, I became part of the royal court, but my humble origins kept me an outsider among the knights."

"I can see why. You have to be of noble blood to become a knight. You seem to have surpassed all the rules of birth simply by the kindness of your heart."

"You have no idea how right you are. I was supposed to stay

at home and inherit my father's farm, but I did a kindness for a traveling stranger and was offered a carpenter's apprenticeship in return. I became an apprentice and my younger brother, who had desperately wanted to be a blacksmith's apprentice, was forced to stay at home with the farm. I suspect he's still mad at me to this day."

"How did you and Aurora meet?"

He chuckled. "As I said, the knights with noble blood wanted nothing to do with me. They were also suspicious of Aurora, who was King Lionel's advisor."

"Why were they suspicious?"

"Because she's a sorceress … a magical being … a creature of legend. She's not human, and therefore, in their minds, not to be trusted. I think the biggest problem they had was even though she looked like she was your age, they had no clue how old she really was."

"How old is she?"

"He has no clue, either," Aurora muttered with a snicker as she moved, trying to get comfortable.

"She could be as old as … 150," he said, trying to prompt her.

"Not even close," she said, weakly crawling across the ground to curl up in his lap. "You take first watch, I'll take second."

He laughed. "Anyway, I didn't care about such silly superstitions, so she and I quickly became friends. This ostracized us even more, but we didn't care. She didn't chastise my quest for knowledge and she even taught me to read. She didn't belittle my belief in God, and I wasn't offended by or afraid of her magic. She even taught me how to use certain magical powders to cast spells in emergency situations."

"Hence the ferret?"

"Exactly." He sighed and glanced down at the ball of fur in his lap, affectionately petting her back. She quickly twisted her body and nipped his finger for his trouble. "Ow!" he exclaimed, sucking on his finger in angst.

"Serves you right," she muttered, changing her position. "I'm not a pet," she grumbled. With that, she finally fell asleep.

"Unfortunately," he continued, "nothing lasts forever. King Lionel's kingdom was sought after by a powerful warlock. He assembled an immortal army to take Lionel's kingdom by force. When the battle broke out, Aurora made a choice. She used every ounce of her magic to protect the two of us, making us impervious to harm and enchanting my sword, but the strain of that kind of magic caused her to collapse. As I fought against enemies that only seemed to fall before my sword, the rest of our people perished. The warlock killed King Lionel personally and then turned his attention on me. He faced me alone, not quite sure how I had withstood his army. In the chaos that followed, I slashed his face with my enchanted sword, cutting his helm and it left a glowing scar across his otherwise flawless face. The warlock became enraged and lashed out at me with magic. I was rendered unconscious and they were able to capture me, just as his henchmen discovered Aurora's unconscious form. He placed Lionel's crown upon his head as he turned his attention to the two of us.

"He was ***upset*** that his army had failed to destroy us, he was ***mad*** I had managed to kill some of his 'immortal' army, but he was ***really furious*** that I had scarred his face. He told us that we would pay dearly for not perishing with our comrades. Using a ***very*** powerful dark magic, he looked into our souls to see how we had been able to withstand his army. He decided that since my good deeds had been what had placed me in his way that day, I would be cursed to do good deeds, a slave to the needs of others, until the end of my days … or until the curse is lifted. Aurora was cursed to spend the rest of her days protecting me since that had been the reason we survived, but if she uses magic to do it for me, she will pay."

"My, that story was changed. Where does the unicorn come in?"

He laughed. "That's a completely different story entirely. We didn't cut the horn off a unicorn. Aurora asked permission of one to obtain a small amount of powder from its horn to counteract the poison from the sting of a manticore. ***I*** never touched the unicorn because I know that a mortal should never come in contact with the pure magic they contain. Aurora used the powder to cure a dying prince and then we were on our way again."

"Is that all? An evil warlock cursed you both to help those who need helping, and she has to protect you? Fate has not been kind to you."

"The Lord watches over me. He will guide me along the path He has chosen for me."

"You do not actually believe in a higher power?"

"I truly believe. If I did not, I wouldn't have made it this far. Besides, aren't you glad we're cursed? If we hadn't been drawn to your cries for help, you might still be in that mirror."

She let out an exasperated sigh. "I suppose you are correct. Goodnight, Sir Christopher. And thank you for the story."

"Goodnight princess."

Chapter IV
A Journey Begins

Gwenyth awoke in the dead of night to the sounds of the forest as the night came alive. When her eyes adjusted to the darkness, she realized that the fire had died down to embers, but she wasn't cold. She turned her head and was astonished to find the warm, furry body of a dark-colored jungle cat pressed up against her. The cat turned its head and blinked its big yellow eyes at her. "Go back to sleep," Aurora's voice soothed, turning back to face the forest. "I've got the watch."

Gwenyth let out the breath that she didn't know she'd been holding and she curled back up against Aurora's soft hide and let sleep overtake her.

Later, when the rosy dawn finally enticed her to open her eyes, she found Christopher packing up the modest camp as if to prepare for a long journey.

"Good morning, Milady," he said cheerily. "Did you sleep well?"

"Better than expected." She glanced around the clearing. "Where is Aurora?"

"Off deciding on the best direction to proceed."

"Which way is north?"

Christopher glanced at the sky. "That direction." He absently pointed off to the left and then went back to packing up their small camp.

"Then that is the best direction to proceed," she said, shuffling her skirts as she tried to gracefully get to her feet.

Christopher raised his eyebrows at her as he tied the bedroll to the back of the saddle. "Pray tell, why is that, Princess?" he asked as he knelt down to don his armor.

"Because that is the direction that home lies." She walked over to Jonathan. "I would like to ride please." When the horse didn't respond, she looked him in the eye with her most endearing smile. "I think you have a very noble name." To Christopher's utter amazement, the large war horse knelt down and allowed her to climb into his saddle.

"What are you doing?" he demanded as he watched his horse get back to his feet with the petite princess perched side-saddle on his back, and it was unclear which of them he was speaking to.

"I am preparing for the journey."

"What journey?!"

"The journey to Aliwyn. Were you really planning to leave me alone to get home by myself?"

Jonathan snorted his own rebuff in Christopher's direction. "Traitor," Christopher growled. The horse tossed his mane in defiance. "Aurora! A little help here!"

The form of a hawk suddenly appeared on the horizon, and Gwenyth began to wonder if Aurora could always hear his cries for help, no matter how trivial or far away.

The hawk flapped her wings and gracefully alighted on a nearby branch. "What's the problem?"

"The princess seems to think that we're taking her home."

Aurora tilted her hawk head and stared at the impatient princess. "Escort duty? With our lifestyle? She'd be better off back in the mirror. At least she couldn't get hurt there."

"My thoughts exactly. Milady, our path is not exactly the safest. You would really be better off on your own than with us."

"I care not. You will protect me from any danger. But I simply refuse to travel to Aliwyn without an escort. It just is not done!"

Christopher rubbed his hands over his face in frustration. "Milady, we can't exactly just pick a direction and go. We must go wherever the magic draws us."

"And unless your home is on the way, we must bid you a fond farewell," Aurora added.

Gwenyth batted her eyes innocently. "Which direction are you going?"

"The magic is drawing me northward."

Christopher sighed in frustration and Gwenyth grinned triumphantly as she turned Jonathan in the right direction and waited for Christopher to follow suit.

He glared at the bird and pointed his finger accusingly. "You are not one of my favorite beings right now!" He shoved his helmet and his breast plate into a bag and tied it to the saddle before climbing up behind Gwenyth, wearing his leg bracers, wrist bracers and chain mail shirt. "Go," he commanded Aurora, his hand outstretched, then he flicked the reins and the horse began to canter in the direction indicated.

"Oops," Aurora whispered, flapping her wings to take to the sky and lead the misfit travelers to their next adventure. "Me and my big … beak."

The next two hours passed slowly, mostly because Christopher was brooding in silence, making Gwenyth very uneasy. Aurora stayed out of sight a majority of that time, reappearing only every once in a while to make sure they were still heading in the right direction. Gwenyth couldn't understand why Christopher hadn't spoken since their day's journey began, and it never occurred to her that he was just used to being alone and not having company when he traveled.

Finally, Gwenyth couldn't stand the silence anymore. "I cannot understand why you are so upset! I have not compelled you to travel out of your way. You were headed this direction anyway."

He let out his breath in a huff. He had been enjoying the serenity of the forest and had almost managed to forget that the loquacious princess was tagging along. "That's not the point. I'm putting you in danger by just having you with me."

She flicked her hair back over her shoulder in annoyance, causing Christopher to sputter in frustration as it hit him full in the face. "I would be in danger traveling alone. What is the harm of traveling with an escort as courageous as yourself?"

"The difference is that by simply traveling with me, I'm putting you in more danger than you would be in if you were by yourself and on foot."

"But you are a knight!" she protested. "How can traveling with you be dangerous?"

"Because trouble always seems to find me!"

From her ladylike position, she turned to give him a supercilious look. "You just do not want a lady along."

He laughed. "You do remember who we're traveling with, don't you?"

She sighed and began speaking in a condescending tone,

"She does not count as a 'lady'. She barely qualifies as a woman. How do you even know that is her true form?"

He tried very hard to conceal a grin. "I don't, I guess. I just trust that Aurora isn't deceiving me."

"You trust too easily."

"You sound like my brother. Forgive me if I see the good in people."

She scoffed and turned back to the forest. "It is so quiet. How do you stand it?"

"You just get used to it after a while. There's a peaceful feeling that comes over me when I'm alone with the sounds of the forest. After six years, I still love the silence. It's comforting."

"Six years? The two of you have been traveling like this for six years? What about your family?"

"I haven't seen my family since I was knighted. And after the battle, we immediately went where the magic was calling. We haven't really stopped since, hence the full suit of armor."

Gwenyth turned back to the forest, wondering how much longer she would have to endure the silence it offered, when Aurora appeared in human form crouched in the middle of the path. "We've got trouble," she gasped, slightly out of breath.

"What kind?" he asked, reaching for his sword.

"Not that kind," she gasped. "There's a farm house on fire. I think … there's people trapped inside."

"Can you get us there?"

With a wave of her hand and a puff of smoke, she magically transported them to the burning farmhouse. Gwenyth watched in horror as Aurora collapsed in a heap on the ground, electricity crackling over her entire body, including the green surface of the talisman she now wore around her neck.

"Are you okay?" he asked as Jonathan knelt down to allow him to dismount. Gwenyth climbed down after him.

Aurora smiled sheepishly. "I've been worse." She struggled to sit up as he knelt down to remove his leg bracers. "The family's still inside. You have to get them out," she wheezed, still short of breath from the spell's backlash.

"Rest!" he commanded as he turned to survey the scene. Gwenyth's heart leapt into her throat as she watched the flames dancing on the walls of the farmhouse, taunting Sir Christopher. The fence surrounding the farm yard was broken and the last of the horses could be seen bolting into the woods. Smoke was billowing out of the upstairs windows of the house and a faint whining sound could be heard over the roar of the flames.

"Get the horses," he said, swatting Jonathan on the flank and sending him off into the woods.

Gwenyth scurried forward with a torn piece of cloth from her skirts. "I used the well water. It should block the smoke."

Christopher looked at her in surprise and then accepted the cloth. "Thank you." He glanced at his guardian. "Wish me luck."

She opened her hand and blew a powder on him, as it was all she had the strength for. "Good luck."

He smiled and then shouldered the smoking door open with a bang and entered the inferno, the two women forced to simply watch and wait.

Chapter V
Before the Flames

Even with the cloth to keep out the smoke, the moment he entered the house he began coughing. The smoke was so thick it could have been cut with a knife. It burned his eyes, causing them to water so badly that he couldn't see and he had to feel his way with his hands.

"Hello!" he called out, slowly making his way across the room. The whining sound had grown louder when he entered the house and he now recognized it as a dog. The dog was somewhere above him, apparently trapped upstairs with the family. He found what remained of a ladder that would lead him to the loft, but there wasn't enough left to hold his weight. "Lord, give me strength," he said aloud as he continued searching for a means of reaching the second floor.

Suddenly, the dog barked, a loud low bark and Christopher was caught off-guard. "How did they get such a big dog up that steep ladder?" he wondered aloud. As he said that, his hand brushed against a rope with a large knot in the end that was hanging from the ceiling. He grabbed the knot and gave it a light tug and was rewarded with a creaking sound above his head. Coming to a conclusion, he gave the rope a good yank and stepped back out of the way. When a loud thump notified him that something had hit the dirt floor, he slowly crept forward, his hands outstretched until he stumbled into another ladder, this one with a more gradual slope to it than the first, almost as gradual as stairs. The dog came bounding down the ladder and began licking his face. Christopher pushed him away and began patting his head.

"Where's your family?" he asked the dog, allowing it to grab him by the wrist and lead him upstairs. The dog barked as it reached the edge of the large bed, and it was answered with the shrieking wail of a baby. Christopher found a small family huddled together on the bed: a mother, a father, a young boy, and the crying infant. He immediately set about getting the family out of the house. He picked up the baby in one arm and threw the young boy over his other shoulder, cautiously starting down the ladder.

As the women waited anxiously for Christopher's reappearance, a piece of the roof collapsed, blocking the doorway with a wall of flames. Gwenyth's heart began to race at this unforeseen complication. Christopher's only means of escaping the inferno and saving the family had just been cut off. She glanced at Aurora in panic. "What do we do?"

"I made him fire-proof, but the smoke will still kill him if he can't get out."

Gwenyth chewed on her lower lip in apprehension as she stared at the blistering inferno. "He has need of an alternate escape route," she grumbled as she spotted an ax protruding from a tree stump in the yard. Setting her jaw in determination, she pried the ax from the stump, but she stumbled and fell over backwards as soon as it was free, sending it flying.

Aurora had to stifle a laugh as the flustered princess got back to her feet. "What ***are*** you doing?"

"I am going to attempt to chop a hole in the wall so he will have an avenue of escape. Care to assist me?"

Aurora's green eyes sparkled with fierce protectiveness and her hair flared to crimson as she began whispering in another language and motioning with her hand at Gwenyth. When she had finished, she only took a moment to admire her handiwork before giving the princess some direction. "Oops! Not quite what I had in mind, but … it'll work. Just swing the ax at the house. You shouldn't have any problems lifting it now."

Gwenyth glanced down and shrieked in disbelief. Her petite feminine form had been transformed into the burly frame of a woodcutter, but her head had remained the same, blonde tresses and all, and she was still wearing the pink and silver gown. The dress had torn in places to accommodate her bulky body and it barely came down past her knees. "Remind me to get mad at you later!" she growled as she hefted the ax onto her shoulder and took a swing.

Christopher reached the bottom of the ladder and was overwhelmed by the heat from the flames that were blocking his exit. "A little help here!" he cried out.

"We're working on it! Head toward the back of the house; there aren't any flames there!" Aurora called.

"No door either!" he yelled as he walked cautiously in the direction indicated.

"Attempting to remedy that!" Gwenyth's strained voice cried out as a section of the wall disappeared beneath the blade of an ax.

He stopped three feet away from the wall and waited as the hole became large enough for him to fit through. As soon as the sunlight began to penetrate the smoky gloom, he stepped forward and passed the squirming infant out into the fresh air to the waiting arms on the other side. He leaned out the hole to hand the young boy out as well, but his eyes narrowed in confusion and his lips pursed in surprise. "What happened to you?"

Gwenyth looked down and frowned while searching for a good explanation. "I made the mistake of asking Aurora for help chopping a hole in the wall."

He shook his head. "You look ridiculous." With that, he disappeared back into the smoke filled house.

"I ***feel*** ridiculous," Gwenyth said, glaring at Aurora as she laid the boy down in the grass next to the squalling infant.

"Hey! I was in a hurry. At least it worked!" Aurora cocked her head to the side and examined her handiwork once again. "You do look ridiculous though."

"Please, tell me you can fix this later."

"Of course," Aurora rolled her eyes in exasperation.

Christopher rushed back up the ladder, shaking his head the whole way. "I never should have left them alone together." He scooped the mother up in his arms and this time the dog followed him down the steps to safety. As he passed the mother out through the hole to the magically enhanced Gwenyth, a loud series of popping and cracking sounds could be heard coming from the ceiling and the nearby walls above them.

"The roof is going to cave in. You must hurry!"

As he turned back into the inferno, Gwenyth was sure she heard him murmur, "God, grant me speed."

Christopher climbed the ladder once again and returned to the family's bedside only to suddenly become very worried. The man must have weighed nearly one hundred pounds more than he did, and he wasn't entirely sure he could lift him, let alone get him down the ladder. "Lord! Lend me your strength!"

"What is taking so long?" Gwenyth demanded of Aurora, but she only shrugged in confusion.

With strength that could not possibly be contained in his body, he jerked the man out of bed and across his shoulders. He gasped in pain as he began the long descent to the floor below. He knew he was running out of time, but he wasn't sure if he had enough strength left to make it out of the building. The walls had been reduced to embers and the structure itself was threatening to fall in on them. He heard the cracking sound that accompanies burning wood as it breaks apart, and he made for the hole at a quicker pace. He reached the hole and struggled to shove the man through to the outside, causing him to land on top of Gwenyth just as the structure caved in on top of him.

"NO!" Aurora cried out in horror. She quickly tried to create a bubble of protection around Christopher as the burning wood fell, but she feared it wasn't in time.

"Help!" Gwenyth yelped, still trapped underneath the man that Christopher had barely rescued.

As they waited in agonizing silence for the dust to clear, Aurora managed to pull Gwenyth out from underneath the unconscious man. When they were both able to turn their attention back to Christopher, they were horrified to discover that there was nothing left of the house but a pile of smoldering wood.

"Chris! Can you hear us?!" Aurora cried in panic.

Woodcutter Gwenyth immediately began pulling wood off the pile, scattering it in all directions. Aurora began flinging the larger pieces, and the ones still too hot to touch, with her magic, all the while frantically calling out to the buried hero.

"I'm alright," his weak response came finally. "But I would be obliged if you could dig me out before the spell wears off and I'm crushed to death."

"It worked," Aurora said, breathing a sigh of relief as she began working harder to clear the rubble.

The pile had soon cooled off enough that the dog began to lend his aide by digging. It took nearly an hour, but they were finally able to extract Sir Christopher from the remains of the house.

"I am in your debt, ladies … as always," he said, the last directed at Aurora.

She smiled briefly and then turned her attention to the now homeless family. "Back to the task at hand."

Christopher knelt on the grass beside the family. The parents and the young boy were unconscious and breathing shallowly, but they were alive. The baby, however, was another story. He was kicking, crying, and squirming all over the place. Christopher gave it one look and then turned to the two women. "What do we do with it?"

Aurora just raised her eyebrows. "What do you mean 'we'? ***I*** have no maternal instincts." She glanced over at the princess. "Let her deal with it. She'll be a mother one day."

Gwenyth glanced down at her oversized woodcutter body. "I am inclined to think I would frighten him like this. Will I be myself again before any inquisitive neighbors show up?"

Aurora laughed. "It should wear off anytime now … but your dress … has definitely seen better days."

"I do not wish to doubt your abilities, but you can conjure me something else to wear? Or can you magically fix this?"

"Well, yes, obviously. I'll fix it once you're back to normal."

"That does not violate your unwritten rules?"

"It shouldn't. It doesn't apply to anything that doesn't help us directly in our quest," Aurora answered, tossing her braid behind her defiantly, her hair once again flaring to scarlet to match her change in temperament.

"Is that normal?" Gwenyth asked.

Aurora cocked her head in surprise and Christopher laughed. "You get used to it. It's kind of an early warning system on her temper. If it turns black, beware the tempest that follows."

"Understood, black is really bad. But then what is really good?"

Christopher shrugged, but Aurora smiled. "Golden yellow."

"Really? I have never seen it that color," he remarked in surprise.

"That tells you something, doesn't it?"

Gwenyth looked confused. "But why does it do that?"

"I'm a magical being … and that means nothing about me is normal."

Gwenyth just shook her head in confusion as she tried to shrug off this disturbing new development.

"Okay, if you ladies can try to revive the family, I will build us a shelter for the night."

Aurora glanced at the sky, then closed her eyes and inhaled slowly. "There's no sign of a storm. We shouldn't actually need a shelter."

He laughed. "Then I will build a fire. You … can watch that," he said, handing the squirming baby to Gwenyth as if it was a potion that he was afraid would explode in his face, before picking up the discarded ax and heading into the forest.

"And I'll set up a spell to watch for nosy neighbors," Aurora said, reaching into a pouch on her belt as she walked away.

"But I..." she began to protest at Aurora's retreating form. "What am ***I*** supposed to do with a baby?" She peered down at the beet red face. Immediately, the baby stopped screaming, batted its eyes twice, cooed, giggled, reached for her hair with its hands, and then hiccupped. "Delightful," she said without enthusiasm.

Chapter VI
Magical Mending

Christopher returned some time later to find Jonathan had managed to round up the horses, and Gwenyth was wrapped in the bed roll from Jonathan's saddle, the sleeping baby curled up in her lap.

"Are you cold?" he asked, watching her pull the blanket in tighter as he approached.

"Uh, no … not exactly," she said, glancing down. "Aurora's spell wore off…"

He narrowed his eyes in confusion.

Aurora appeared out of the forest at that moment, a large bow strung over one shoulder, a quiver of arrows over the other, and two rabbits grasped in her left hand. "I brought dinner." She looked up as she approached the fire and caught the strange look on Christopher's face. "What did I miss?"

"Your spell wore off," Gwenyth replied meekly.

"OH!" Aurora exclaimed, her eyes going wide and her hair rippling orange in embarrassment. "Chris, turn around!"

He happily complied and waited for Aurora to give him the all clear, glancing at the surrounding forest. Aurora sprinkled a fine grained yellow powder on Gwenyth's dress, whispered a few unintelligible words and stepped back to watch as the dress seemed to stitch itself back together.

As soon as the magic was complete, Gwenyth breathed a

sigh of relief as she examined her dress. "Thank goodness that is over."

"Can I turn around now?" Christopher asked hesitantly.

Aurora laughed. "All clear."

He turned around and examined his companions. "Was she really that small before?"

"What?!" the petite princess shrieked. "You made me smaller?!"

Aurora pushed her fingers into the center of her forehead and slowly began massaging from the bridge of her nose to the line of her hair. "Chris, cut it out."

He laughed. "I'm kidding. You're fine. I'm still not sure why that happened, though."

"I'm just having an off day … and I think I'm getting a headache."

"A 'head-ache'? What is that?" Gwenyth asked.

"Something your descendants will become very familiar with."

Christopher cocked his head at her. "Natural or mystical?"

She smiled at him. "Natural … and therefore a human ailment."

"You have been hanging out with me too long … especially if it's beginning to undo … oh … 200 years of conditioning."

She smiled. "Not even close."

He laughed. "Can't blame a guy for trying. Well, ladies, you had better get some sleep. We do have a family to revive in the morning."

"You take first?" Aurora asked, cocking her head.

He nodded. "See you in five."

Gwenyth silently watched their exchange and found herself wondering what it was they weren't saying that they both just seemed to know. She curled up with the baby near the fire, and eventually fell asleep while watching Christopher on sentry duty.

Aurora's internal alarm went off exactly five hours later. She rolled onto her hands and knees, shaking and stretching in a feline posture, her body slowly morphing into that of a large jungle cat.

"It has been quiet," Christopher muttered as he lay down beside her, using the heat from her fur covered body to keep warm.

"See you in five," she said quietly, turning her glowing yellow eyes on the forest.

Gwenyth stirred during the night and startled herself awake, slightly alarmed at the sight of Sir Christopher crouched by the unconscious family with his sword drawn. She rubbed the sleep from her eyes, hoping that would help them adjust to the darkness a little quicker. She glanced around the clearing again, and a lump formed in her throat when she realized that Aurora was nowhere to be seen. Christopher was next to the young boy, his right hand outstretched and hovering over the boy in a protective gesture, his eyes scanning the edge of the clearing, presumably for Aurora's reappearance.

When the sinewy black cat finally did slink out of the forest, both Gwenyth and Christopher breathed sighs of relief.

"False alarm," she purred, walking past Christopher soundlessly. He reached out and patted her on the head and then put his sword away, turning to follow her back to their chosen point of vigilance. Gwenyth was certain that she saw the big cat roll its eyes in apathy in response to the knight's gesture of affection.

Gwenyth settled back in for the rest of the night, and as she nodded off, she felt incredibly secure. For her, knowing that Christopher and Aurora were a seamless team, alert and prepared for anything, made even the dangers of the forest seem no more frightening than if she were tucked in her down bed at home.

Chapter VII
A Friendship Revealed

As the rising sun finally found a way to penetrate her rather heavy eyelids, Gwenyth awoke to discover that the family had regained consciousness. Christopher and the father were examining the remains of the farmhouse while the mother was helping her children to eat their breakfast. Gwenyth smoothed her skirts and hair before she approached the mother and children to see if she could be of some assistance.

"There were always whispered tales of a knight who helps those in need, doing heroic deeds with little regard for his own safety, but I never believed there was any truth to the tales," the mother said, glancing at Sir Christopher with admiration.

Gwenyth followed the woman's gaze and smiled to herself. Only two days before, she had felt the same way, and now that she knew the truth she could ***still*** scarcely believe it.

"Ah, the lady stirs," Christopher said as he and the father rejoined the circle. He handed her a piece of bark with a strange piece of bread, some berries and some roasted meat on it. "This is Princess Gwenyth, and without her help I'm afraid we would all have been roasted alive."

"What a pleasant thought," she said, examining her breakfast with disdain thanks to his comment.

"A lady of the court who accompanies you?" the father asked in a perplexed tone. "Highly irregular."

"Actually, it is the other way around," Gwenyth replied

with a smile, setting aside her unappetizing breakfast. "He rescued me from a rather terrible ordeal. There was a wizard that just would not take no for an answer. Now he is helping me to return home." Out of the corner of her eye, she noticed that Christopher made a face in frustration, but she didn't let that bother her. "It appears, however, that our other companion has vanished."

"You have another knight traveling with you?" the father asked in bewilderment.

Christopher laughed. "Not quite. Aurora will be back shortly, I'm sure. She's just off alerting your neighbors to your plight."

"She is kind of his mischievous guardian angel. She will conveniently reappear when she is needed."

Sir Christopher glared at her. "Something like that." He turned his head so that only Gwenyth could hear and hissed through clenched teeth under his breath, "Strange that a lady of breeding does not know when to hold her tongue."

Gwenyth sucked in a breath, realizing that Christopher had not intended to mention Aurora at all.

"A guardian angel? Sounds like sorcery to me," the father murmured, drawing his small family closer to him as if to protect them from evil.

Gwenyth bent her head over her food as she tried to hide her guilt and embarrassment. It dawned on her that she had been allowed into their tight-knit world because of her exposure to magic in her kidnapping, but most people they encountered weren't. Whereas she had ultimately been intrigued by the magical elements of their stories, most people would be frightened by it. This poor family would find that

Christopher's story was full of superstitions and they would probably feel that Aurora was not to be trusted because she was a magical being. Her thoughts drifted back to Christopher's story of how he had met Aurora and the reactions of the other knights in Lionel's court, and she suddenly felt that she had forced her presence upon the accursed travelers, disrupting their natural dynamic.

"Does she partake of the black arts?" the mother asked, drawing Gwenyth back into the conversation.

"Is she contracted with the devil?" the young boy asked, fear and awe in his tone.

"Mind your tongue!" the mother reprimanded. "She will put a hex on us!"

Christopher sighed in frustration. "Help ... anytime..." Gwenyth heard him mutter, as if he'd been saying it all along.

Gwenyth straightened up, her eyes scanning the line of trees, waiting for Aurora's impeccable timing to present itself. As if on cue, the dog barked and rushed off as Aurora's huntress form stepped from the tree line, looking anything but the part of a sorceress. She had her hair tied back in a braid, and the brilliant green of her tunic offset the natural-looking strawberry blonde of her hair perfectly. She had a bow and quiver of arrows at her back and she was leading a horse and cart. She patted the dog on the head as he playfully ran around her legs.

"Finally!" Christopher called out, the joy and relief apparent in his voice. He stood up and walked over to meet her. "About time!" he hissed under his breath. "What kept you?"

"Would you prefer I'd shown up without a cover story?" she replied through the clenched teeth of her fake smile that she had donned for the small audience that was watching from the clearing. He breathed a heavy sigh of frustration, causing a genuine smile to cross her lips. "You can thank me later," she said, patting his chest as she passed.

As they approached the silent audience, Aurora smiled at them each in turn. She tied a weight to the horse's bridle and got him to graze near Jonathan. "Your neighbors sent a few supplies they thought you would need right now and they plan to follow shortly. They said it was strange because they never smelled the smoke."

Christopher crossed his legs and seemed to gracefully fold himself into a sitting position. "It *was* rather windy last night. The smoke probably dissipated as it cleared the trees."

"I'm glad to see that the morning has found you in better health," Aurora said, still smiling.

"Much better, thank you," the father said, returning her smile.

Gwenyth had to concentrate to keep her mouth from falling open in surprise. Where only moments before the family had been ready to condemn a sorceress, they now had completely accepted the huntress who had gone to enlist help from the neighbors. Aurora flicked her braid behind her shoulders as she began unloading clothing and blankets from the cart. She winked in Gwenyth's direction as she set down some of the bundles, and Gwenyth couldn't believe her eyes. She glanced over at Christopher and saw him smiling at his associate. In that moment, Gwenyth realized that they had probably planned this in case of exposure. She made a promise to herself not to speak of things unless Christopher spoke first, and to detach herself as soon as possible from the adventurers.

The family took time to change into the clean clothes provided by Aurora's mercy mission, and shortly thereafter the neighbors came wandering out of the forest from all directions. The men were carrying tools of all kinds and the women and children were carrying food and any household necessities they could spare. Gwenyth did her best to fade into the background as she watched Christopher and Aurora work together to get the family and their neighbors organized. Once a plan of action for rebuilding the farm and taking care of the family was established, the heroes took their leave and continued on their journey.

Chapter VIII
Earning a Name

As they left the family behind to rebuild their life, a feeling of dread began forming in the pit of Gwenyth's stomach. Aurora had gone ahead in huntress form to scout where the magic was drawing them, and Christopher was walking alongside Jonathan while the princess rode. She glanced down at him in concern. "Which direction are we headed in now?"

He glanced at the sky. "East, it appears. Why do you ask?"

"It does not feel right. It feels dark."

He sighed. "Welcome to my world." He glanced around the forest for witnesses before calling out, "Aurora! Assistance!"

She appeared before them in a puff of white smoke. "Already? We just barely got started again."

He laughed. "Gwenyth feels uneasy. She says that the direction we're heading in feels dark."

Aurora raised her eyebrows in mild annoyance, her hair shimmering purple for a second. "Well, when the magic draws us to our next quest, if our quest is to be against a powerful magical foe, the air gets heavier with dark magic the closer we get. ***Normally*** humans can't sense the difference."

Gwenyth shivered as the meaning of Aurora's words struck her. "I did not even believe in magic until Varuk trapped me in that mirror, and now you are telling me that I can sense it?"

"An unexpected side-effect of your out of control spell, I take it?" he asked, glancing back and forth between the women.

Aurora's temper flared, sending jet black tendrils of color through her already burgundy colored hair, and Gwenyth's eyes went wide with fright. Aurora took a slow controlled breath and seemed to stare right through Christopher. "I love how I am automatically the one to blame for everything mystical that occurs! That's a convenient way to go about things: Everything is Aurora's fault!" Her voice was slowly increasing in volume and the black was spreading through her hair. Jonathan jerked his head back to remove his reins from Christopher's clenched fist and galloped into the trees, spiriting Gwenyth away from the potential danger of the sorceress' rage. "I have an off day and suddenly you blame me for everything! I suggest you watch yourself or I'll make you take this next creature on alone!" The talisman hanging around her neck was slowly glowing brighter green. The intensity of the light increased with her volume and by the time Christopher noticed it, it was glowing as bright as a full moon.

"Uh, Aurora?" he said, trying to break her tirade.

"Maybe next time I won't be there to bail you out and then you'll appreciate everything I do to help!" she screeched, and with a flash of green light, she vanished.

"Oh, not good!" Christopher muttered, eyes wide in panic as he spun around to search the surrounding forest. "Aurora! Aurora, this isn't funny! Get back here!"

A loud scream suddenly echoed through the trees, followed by a horse's terrified shriek. "Gwenyth!" he yelled, drawing his sword and racing off through the trees, silently praying he'd make it in time.

"Christopher!" Aurora shrieked, trying desperately to make him hear her. She watched as he ran off to the rescue, the green haze that surrounded her rippling in his wake. "What's going on?!"

The hazy green mist rippled again and suddenly she was standing in the forest, twenty feet from Princess Gwenyth, who had been thrown from Jonathan's back and was lying unconscious in a heap at the base of a tree. Jonathan was reared up on his hind legs, flailing his front legs defensively at a seven foot tall Cyclops. A young female centaur was lying nearby, her hands bound and a lasso tied around all four hooves. She was whimpering and crying, but there was nothing Aurora could do for any of them. The green mist that surrounded her was preventing her from moving, and all she could do was watch and hope Christopher could handle it on his own.

Christopher came running into the clearing full tilt with his sword drawn, but he skidded to a halt when he discovered what he was up against. The Cyclops licked his lips greedily when his eye caught sight of Christopher, alone, armed only with a sword and wearing no armor.

"Aurora!" he yelled in panic as he dove to avoid the Cyclops' outstretched hands and rolled out of the way, trying desperately to reach Jonathan and his armor.

The Cyclops grunted and called out something in another language, grinning evilly.

"Now what?" the valiant knight asked, taking a defensive stance as he scanned the trees trying to prepare himself for what was coming. The centaur let out a horrified shriek and began to struggle against her bonds, but to no avail.

As Christopher tried to watch every direction at once, six armed bandits stepped from the trees: three carrying swords, one with a bow and arrows, one with a bolo, and one with a net. The three with swords immediately began advancing on Sir Christopher, eager to kill the heroic knight.

"God protect me," he whispered as he breathed a sigh of frustration and stepped into the fray. He ducked under the first bandit's lunge and crossed swords with the second. The third tried to catch him from behind, but he side-stepped and used the second bandit's sword to catch the attack.

Aurora could do nothing but watch in fear. Christopher pivoted to his right and elbowed the first attacker in the head, stunning him and knocking him to the ground. He heard the twang of an arrow being released from a bow, so he finished swinging around to face his enemies and ducked as an arrow sailed past him and got stuck in a tree.

Aurora let out an uncontrolled yelp as the arrow barely missed his unprotected skin. The fourth bandit was stringing another arrow and waiting for an unobstructed shot at Christopher, while the fifth bandit used his bolo to finally bring Jonathan to his knees. She set her jaw in determination; if she was powerless to help Christopher, she'd just have to make sure that Gwenyth wasn't. The sixth bandit had just finished securing a net over the unconscious princess and Aurora's eyes darted around the clearing, desperately searching for an answer. *I am a powerful sorceress,* she thought to herself. *I can think of a spell to wake her up.* Suddenly, an idea struck her; she shut her eyes and began whispering to the wind in Gaelic.

Christopher lunged at the second and third attackers, deflecting the second one's sword off to the left as he stepped forward to elbow him in the head. He then reached down with his right hand and yanked his attacker's sword free, turning and swinging both swords at his third adversary. The bandit staggered backwards under Christopher's attack just as the sky was lit with a brilliant bolt of lightning and followed closely by a resounding crash of thunder. Christopher's eyes went wide as the skies seemed to simply open and dump an entire lake's worth of water on the clearing. In the midst of the torrential downpour, Christopher forced the third bandit's sword to the ground with his left sword and brought his right arm back to swing over his shoulder. The fourth bandit released another arrow, and this time Christopher wasn't quick enough. The arrow embedded itself in the back of his right shoulder and he cried out in pain, just as the Cyclops, who had been patiently biding his time, lunged forward and grabbed Christopher's right wrist, yanking him over backwards into the mud. The arrow's shaft snapped as he landed flat on his back, but not before forcing the arrowhead through his shoulder blade. He cried out in pain as his borrowed sword went flying out of his right hand, and the Cyclops quickly stepped on his left wrist, pinning it into the mud with his sword still clenched in his fist. *Well, at least she's trying to help, wherever she is,* he thought briefly, knowing that the spiteful sorceress was behind the bizarre weather phenomenon.

Gwenyth's eyes had darted open the moment the icy rain had hit her. She had glanced around in panic, trying desperately to figure out what was going on. She had let out a yelp as Christopher got shot and landed in the mud, attracting the attention of the sixth bandit. He stepped forward, greedily reaching for the princess, his eyes bulging out of his head at the sight of her terrified face. She opened her mouth and let out a blood-curdling scream that echoed to every corner of the forest. The Cyclops staggered away from Christopher, both hands clasped over his ears; Christopher let go of his sword to protect his ears from the horrible shriek; and the bandits all fell to their knees and covered their ears, trying desperately to block out the noise.

Aurora couldn't even move in order to cover her ears, so she was forced to endure Gwenyth's scream full blast from only twenty feet away. "Ugh! He thought I was kidding about the shrill! Shrill was an understatement!"

The female centaur began to add an excited cry to Gwenyth's scream, causing the Cyclops to writhe on the ground in agony. From his position on the ground, Christopher could feel the rumble long before anyone could actually hear it over Gwenyth's scream. He rolled to his side and trained his eyes on the tree line, anxiously awaiting whatever this new threat might be. By the time the roar overpowered the screech, he was able to identify it as the pounding of hooves. He watched as a huge herd of centaurs, numbering more than thirty, began pouring out of the forest. Gwenyth stopped screaming at the sight of the centaurs, and the bandits grabbed their discarded weapons, quickly and unceremoniously fleeing back into the trees. Several of the centaurs pursued the Cyclops as he fled the area.

Christopher picked himself up out of the mud, his right arm hanging limply as he sheathed his sword with his left. He staggered over to Gwenyth and began to free her from her bonds, trying desperately to remain conscious.

"Goodness, I am glad that is over!" Gwenyth sighed as he managed to untangle her from the net that held her captive. As those words left her mouth, a flash of green light signaled Aurora's reappearance.

"Where have you been?!?!" Christopher demanded at the sight of her. She slid under his left arm to support him and nodded at Gwenyth to get her to help the young centaur.

"Don't ask," she said, helping him to sit.

The young centaur let out a strange sound to Gwenyth's ears as she got to her feet and rushed into the open arms of the nearest centaur. The head of the centaur clan approached Aurora. "Noble-Heart, I presume?"

She looked up in surprise. "It's been a very long time since anyone has called me that."

He smiled at her. "While my father may not still be with us, the kindness you did for him will never fade. The *Landoc* clan shall always know your name."

"What are they talking about?" Gwenyth whispered, kneeling next to Sir Christopher.

He shook his head. "Whatever it is, it was before I knew her."

"We are once again in your debt for having returned the young one to us," the centaur chief continued. "She had wandered off and no doubt would have become a trophy in the Dark Lord's castle if you had not happened by."

Aurora shivered involuntarily. "Actually, you have Sir Christopher of Calidore to thank for the young one's rescue. I was … occupied elsewhere and unable to get here until just after your arrival."

"Sir Christopher? You travel with a knight?"

She smiled. "We're … partners, after a fashion."

The centaur chief bowed to Sir Christopher, who did his best to return the gesture from the ground while clutching his wounded shoulder. The chief turned to his clan and shouted something in the centaur language, raising his hands in a triumphant gesture. When he finished, each member of the clan bowed to Sir Christopher, even the young one. The chief then turned back to the humans. "From this day forward, Sir Christopher of Calidore, you shall be known as *Grahuual*, Gracious-Protector, to the *Landoc* clan. We thank you from the bottom of our souls, and we shall always remember your deeds. But we must now return to our haven. The world of men is no place for us." He pressed his open right hand to his lips and then turned it palm out to the humans in a farewell gesture. "May the journey protect you."

"May the journey protect you," Aurora answered, mimicking his hand gesture. With that, the centaur clan vanished into the surrounding forest.

"They gave me a new name?" he asked as Aurora approached and began to examine his shoulder.

"It's an honor to be given a name by the centaurs. Names in our language don't translate, so those they deem of enough importance are renamed in their language. To them, I am known as *Nabayla*, or Noble-Heart as it translates." She shook her head at his wound, trying to clear the mud away.

"The centaur we saved, why didn't they refer to her by name?" Gwenyth asked, wringing the water from her curly hair.

Aurora sighed in frustration as she pressed her fingers into the wound and Christopher jerked away in pain. "The centaurs believe that a name should reflect who you are, so the clan gives the newer members their names after a defining moment in their young lives. Until that moment takes place, they are simply known as 'the young ones'. A strange tradition, but it has survived for a millennium." She removed her oil-skin bag from Jonathan's saddle and poured some of the liquid over Christopher's wound.

"That's making me ill!" Gwenyth exclaimed, turning away from the strange sight. The liquid was actually beginning to foam, causing it to turn red and black with the dirt and blood it was removing from the wound. Then, it began to congeal, creating an impenetrable seal over the wound.

"Well, that will do for now, but we need a place to stop where I can clean this properly and then heal you."

"We also need to figure out how the talisman works so that ***this*** doesn't happen again." He winced and then turned to the princess. "When Aurora accidentally transformed you into a woodcutter, was the talisman around her neck glowing bright green?"

The princess cocked her head to the side and her face took on a pensive look as she thought back to the night before, and Aurora nearly burst out laughing because it looked more comical than thoughtful. "I believe it was, now that you mention it. Why do you ask?"

"Because it was glowing bright green right before she disappeared and couldn't get back to help."

"Hey! I helped!" Aurora protested.

"Yeah, and I ***still*** got shot. I would like to avoid a repeat."

Aurora stared at the ground, a crestfallen look on her face. "Well, Lysette lives only half a league from here. I'm sure she could help us unlock the mysteries of the talisman."

Christopher sucked in a breath. "She doesn't like me very much."

"She doesn't like any human very much. Don't take it personally."

"Who is Lysette?" Gwenyth asked, getting Jonathan to kneel down next to Christopher. Gwenyth climbed up into the saddle and reached her hand back to help Christopher get up behind her while Aurora steadied him from behind.

"Lysette is a sorceress. She taught me everything I know about magic." After Christopher was situated, Aurora transformed into her favorite traveling form, the hawk. "Follow me and we should be there by nightfall." With that, she soared high overhead to lead them in the direction of Lysette's.

Gwenyth let a giggle slip. "She must really hate to walk."

"You have no idea," he responded, clicking his tongue and spurring Jonathan in the direction Aurora had flown.

Chapter IX
Discovering Green Fury

The journey to Lysette's was rather uneventful, leading them to a particularly dense patch of forest far away from everything. As the trees began to press in closer and closer, Gwenyth glanced at Christopher uneasily. "Is Lysette dangerous?"

He let out a forced laugh. "Dangerous? That depends. She's a magical being; she feels that humans are weak, that they corrupt everything they touch, and that all magical beings should abstain from getting involved in human affairs. She hates me because somehow it's my fault that Aurora is stuck in this curse with me."

"Is she evil?"

He shook his head. "It would be so much easier to deal with her if she was. Evil I know how to fight. Lysette prides herself on the fact that she's neutral in the fight of good versus evil. Every once in a while she steps in to help one side or the other; however, her help is never one-sided. But, no, she's not evil."

"Is she going to hate me?"

He laughed. "No, ***you*** she will probably ignore. You should be fine."

Gwenyth turned her eyes back to the forest that was now so close that she could have stretched out her hands and touched the branches on both sides simultaneously. She and Christopher had to duck every few moments to avoid being hit in the face by a low hanging tree branch, and even Jonathan had to duck on occasion.

Finally, the narrow path they were on seemed to simply dead-end at a large, gnarled tree. They found Aurora crouched down in front of the trunk, whispering in Gaelic. "*Caraidean*!" she commanded in a louder tone. As the final word left her mouth, a dense fog arose to conceal the tiny clearing. Jonathan knelt to allow Christopher and Gwenyth to dismount rather clumsily, since Christopher was still favoring his injured right shoulder.

Aurora turned to her companions. "Come down with me. Don't worry about Jonathan. The fog will conceal him."

Christopher sighed in defeat and it was in that moment that Gwenyth realized where they were going. The large tree roots appeared to have pulled themselves out of the ground on one side of the tree and moved aside to reveal a vast opening that descended down into the earth beneath the gnarled tree roots. "We are going down there?" Gwenyth whimpered.

Christopher gave her a little nudge of encouragement before stepping past her and following Aurora down into the darkness. "She won't bite!" he called back to Gwenyth. The princess stood in the fog staring at the lacuna, where a staircase was now visible, for a few moments before reluctantly deciding to follow Sir Christopher down into the dark.

As she descended into the earth, Gwenyth felt the strength of the magic within the place growing, filling her with unease all over again. Twice she nearly turned around to go back up and wait with Jonathan, but her curiosity got the better of her. Moisture hung heavily in the air, making it feel almost as if she was drinking every breath.

"Ahh! The prodigal daughter returns!" a sickly sweet melodic voice called out as they reached the bottom. Aurora had already waltzed into the room beyond the staircase, but Christopher had stopped in the doorway, so Gwenyth was forced to peer around him to see into the dimly lit room. To her surprise, the woman standing next to Aurora didn't appear any older than she was. She was dressed in a lavish purple robe, her blonde hair piled on top of her head in an elaborate twisted knot, and she was eagerly bent over a workbench examining the talisman, conversing with Aurora in whispered tones.

"Are you going to lurk in my doorway all day or are you going to come inside and get cleaned up?" Lysette glanced up to fix her icy blue eyes on Christopher's pained face.

He took a deep breath and then slowly entered the sorceress' lair. Gwenyth followed close on his heels, her eyes nervously darting about trying to get a feel for her new surroundings.

"Aurora, you better get your hero patched up. I'll see what I can make of your new trinket."

Aurora nodded her head in agreement as she steered Sir Christopher to a chair in the corner. She forced him to pull off his tunic and then began cleaning his wound more thoroughly than she had been able to while they were on the road. Gwenyth could do nothing but gape at the symphony of ugly scars that were scattered all over his bare torso. He winced in pain every time Aurora's fingers came in contact with the open wound.

"This is going to hurt," she warned him as she concentrated on the arrowhead. Suddenly, she flicked her wrist and sent the arrowhead flying out the front of his chest to land with a soft thud on the packed dirt floor.

"Argh!" he cried out, doubling over in pain.

"Don't be such a baby!" she said, pressing her palm into his new wound to stop the bleeding.

"You left the arrowhead in him?" Lysette asked, calmly glancing up from her task. Her tone turned stern. "Don't bleed on my floor."

"Thank you for your concern," he hissed. Aurora pulled a pinch of purple powder from a jar on a nearby shelf, sprinkled it on each side of the wound in his shoulder, rubbed her hands together and pressed her hands on the opening, one hand front and back. He grunted in pain as she applied pressure, but a warm glow began radiating from her hands and he soon sighed in relief.

She stepped back to admire his newest scar as Christopher moved and flexed his shoulder, rotating it to make sure he had full range of motion again. "Very nice," he said, nodding in approval of her handiwork.

She handed him a clean tunic and smiled. "Always good to know I haven't lost my touch."

Lysette glanced up with a disapproving look on her face as Christopher pulled the new tunic on over his head. "A touch you should never have bothered with in the first place." Aurora sighed and rolled her eyes in frustration. "Don't give me that look, young lady!"

Aurora smiled sweetly and approached her mentor. "Have you made any progress?"

Lysette gave her a reproachful look before leaning back over the talisman. She sprinkled some green powder on the jewel's face and watched as the powder burst into flame as it came in contact with the jewel, and a net of energy began crackling around the talisman. "Somebody doesn't want us playing with his toys while he's away."

"Yeah, his castle vanished into thin air too."

Lysette snorted in disapproval. "Watchdog spells! You don't need them if you avoid living among humans!" She turned to the shelf behind her and grabbed another jar of powder. When that too burst into flame, she frowned. "Well, at least it's only a basic watchdog spell. He apparently didn't think anyone with real magical training would get their hands on this. No offense, my dear."

"None taken," Aurora replied, a small smile gracing her lips.

Christopher settled into his chair, stretching his legs out in front of him and crossing his ankles, folding his arms over his chest and allowing his head to drop in slumber. Gwenyth found herself wandering around the circular room, examining all of the magical wonders and trinkets the shelves displayed so openly.

Lysette glanced up at the silent princess. "She looks like you plucked her from a river. That won't do at all. Aurora, go see if my wardrobe is willing to give her a more suitable dress. Something that befits her station."

Gwenyth nervously met the older sorceress' gaze and curtsied in her most regal way. "I thank you for your generosity."

Lysette made a hissing sound in annoyance. "Generosity, bah. I'm just fixing the balance that Aurora destroyed with her little water show. Besides, I don't want you tracking any more mud on my floor!"

Aurora attempted to stifle a giggle as she led the bedraggled princess through the only other door in the room.

"She does know that it is a dirt floor?"

"Yeah. Don't ask, because I'm not sure I could even begin to explain it." The room they had entered was a very simple bedroom, and Aurora positioned Gwenyth directly in front of the wardrobe. "After a thousand years, apparently you pick up a few eccentricities." She turned to the wardrobe. "Formal wear," she commanded.

"She is a thousand years old?!" Gwenyth exclaimed, reaching to open the wardrobe doors when Aurora indicated.

"Uh ... 1206 actually. Do you fancy any of these?"

Gwenyth gazed at the finery the wardrobe had produced. "They are all my size!"

"Just like magic. Imagine that," Aurora said, sarcasm heavy in her tone, but the princess missed it. She was too busy examining the dresses.

Gwenyth stepped behind the changing screen with a pale blue gown and began to strip off her travel-soiled dress. "If she is 1206, how old are you?"

Aurora laughed. "You're starting to sound like Chris."

"I shall not tell him, I swear!"

Aurora shook her head. "You can just forget it. I'm not letting that secret get out."

Gwenyth let her breath out in a huff. "If you are keeping it such a secret, it must be good. You must be 500 or more."

"Oh!" Aurora said, surprised by the sudden reappearance of the princess' spunk. "I was beginning to wonder when we'd see this side of you again."

Gwenyth stepped from behind the screen. "Can you lace me up? I have never done this without help before."

Aurora rolled her eyes and sighed, her hair rippling orange before quickly returning to its normal brilliant shade of blood red. Her nimble fingers quickly tightened the laces on the elaborate gown. "We better hurry up. I hate leaving Chris alone with Lysette for too long. She might turn him into a frog or something, depending on her mood."

"Can you do that? Enchant people, I mean."

Aurora smiled a rather wicked grin. "You saw what I did to you … and that was by accident. Imagine what I can do on purpose." With that, Aurora turned and left the room.

Gwenyth's eyes went wide as her imagination took over. She picked up her skirts and scampered after her. "Really?"

Aurora walked back into the common room, laughing the whole time. Lysette looked up in disdain. "Did the mortal say something to amuse you?"

Aurora stopped laughing and glared at her mentor with a pitying smirk on her face. "Always. You should try conversing with them instead of commanding them sometime. They might surprise you."

"Doubtful. Besides, I'm better at commanding. I thought you had that figured out after the first hundred years."

"Which is why I spent the next hundred ignoring your commands."

Lysette sighed. "I'm so glad you grew out of that stage. Although, now you just choose not to listen to me."

"I am no longer your apprentice. I don't have to listen to you anymore. Others have shown me that."

"And look where that got you! Don't even get me started on that lousy decision!"

Aurora turned her back on her mentor so that she wouldn't see her roll her eyes, but her hair rippled purple for a second.

"I saw that, young lady!" Lysette glanced around and fixed her eyes on Christopher's sleeping form. "Christopher! I know you're not really sleeping. Open your hand!"

He slowly opened one eye and uncrossed his arms so that he could open his left hand. A small gold key with a scarlet ribbon appeared in his open palm and he shifted his weight in the chair so that he could get to his feet. "And what would you have me do with this, Madam?"

"In the library is a small green cupboard against the far wall. Bring me the two books bound in red dragon skin that are inside."

Christopher smiled submissively, bowed slightly and walked to the same door that the ladies had just returned through, winking at Aurora as he passed. Gwenyth's forehead creased in confusion as he neared the door because she couldn't remember seeing any other way out of the bedroom. However, when he opened it, instead of seeing the bedroom she had just come out of, there were wall-to-wall books on the other side.

Gwenyth watched in awe as Christopher stepped through the doorway into the library and closed the door behind him. She quickly walked over to the door and opened it herself, but she let out a shriek and her jaw slid open in a very unladylike fashion because the door had opened to a swirling emptiness that sucked at her loose hair and skirts, trying to pull her into the void.

Lysette glanced up when she heard Gwenyth's cry. "If you don't close the door, he can't get back," she said patronizingly.

Gwenyth's eyes went wide in horror as she quickly shut the door and scurried out of the way so that he could get back. She was about to voice her exasperation over the whole thing when the door opened and Christopher returned with the requested books.

"Your books and key, Madam," he said, bowing slightly as he placed the items on the workbench near her.

"Thank you, my dear Christopher. That will be all." She opened her hand and the book on top floated into her open palm.

Christopher turned and headed back to his chair. He caught Gwenyth's eye as he passed. "Close your mouth. An enchantress would obviously have an enchanted house. They take up less room."

"But … but … the door! It doesn't go anywhere!"

Christopher laughed as he settled back into his chair. "It only goes somewhere when Lysette wants it to."

Another flash of green light drew their attention back to the conversation between the two magic wielders.

"What did you say the name of the owner of this marvelous talisman is?" Lysette asked as she picked it up and gazed at the fist sized stone set in the ornate gold setting, surrounded by foreign symbols.

"Varuk," Aurora answered.

"Oh, no. Not that simpleton. He doesn't know enough about magic to be responsible for this. No, he had to have help. The Dark Lord, maybe … or a powerful warlock. But he couldn't do it alone."

Aurora glared at her mentor at the mention of the dark lord, and Christopher visibly shuddered and took a deep breath at the mention of a warlock. "What does that mean?" he asked.

"It means that Varuk is worthless without this talisman. He's getting up there in years and his magical ability is nowhere near what it should be. He probably went crawling back to his master for something else the moment he lost this. The talisman amplifies the powers of the person who wears it, which is why your ***powers*** seemed a little out of control."

"Well, I know you saw what happened," Aurora paused, rather annoyed by this time, "so what's wrong with it?"

Lysette laughed. "Why must you assume the talisman is to blame for your faulty magic? There's nothing wrong with it. You're just over-emotional."

"I beg your pardon!"

"Oh, don't get upset, you'll just prove my point. See, this is what comes from fraternizing with humans. Magical beings aren't supposed to feel human emotion, you know this!"

"Oh, so you're saying this is my fault!"

"Aurora, calm down," Christopher pleaded as a thin stripe of black appeared in her hair.

"The talisman feeds off emotion. If the wearer is in complete control of their emotions, then they are in complete control of the talisman. Because you are ruled by your emotions, the talisman has taken on a mind of its own."

Gwenyth laughed, and Christopher turned to glare at her. She quickly hid her smile.

Lysette continued. "Let me guess. Every time you experienced some sort of magical backlash, it was right after you got emotional about something?"

Gwenyth nodded, but Aurora kept her mouth shut, her emotions beginning to seethe just below the surface.

"Whatever emotions you were feeling at the time," the older sorceress said, flinging the train of her robe behind her dramatically as she spun to face the travelers, "those emotions were strong enough to overpower the watchdog spell that is supposed to keep anyone but its owner from using it."

"So, how am I supposed to use it intentionally?" Aurora asked crossly.

"Simple ... *Brách Solais.*" The talisman began to glow bright green, casting eerie shadows into the far corners of the room. A half smile spread across Aurora's face, Christopher stood up out of his chair in wonder, and Gwenyth's mouth fell open in utter amazement. Lysette smiled at them graciously, masking her disdain for their sense of awe. "The talisman will now amplify the powers of the one who wears it. With Varuk, that amplification was more than 100 times in order to give him some semblance of power. I have no idea what it will do for you, my dear, but I suggest you exercise caution. It's entirely possible that if you use the talisman now that the watchdog spell is gone, its creator will be able to track it, and you won't want to run into its creator."

"If it can help us, that's a chance we'll have to take," Aurora replied curtly, snatching the talisman off the bench and replacing it around her neck.

"Remember, if you continue to allow yourself to be ruled by your emotions, then the talisman will not work the way you want it to. You will constantly feel as if you are out of control." She gave Aurora a disapproving look. "If you can't keep your emotions in check, it will continue to enhance your powers randomly when your emotions are in flux. When you lose control, there's no telling what may happen with your magic."

"Are you done lecturing? I'm not your apprentice anymore; I don't have to put up with this!"

"Well, maybe if you'd listened to me when you were my apprentice, we wouldn't be having this conversation!"

"You can't tell me what to do anymore! I haven't needed you to tell me what to do for more then one hundred years, so don't start now!"

"Look! You're losing control, just like you always do when you let emotion in. I don't know where you learned that. It certainly wasn't from me."

"Emotion is an important part of humans and their interaction! Without it, what good is it to be alive?!"

"And with it you will not remain so! Are their lives more important than yours?"

"Ladies, please!" Christopher interjected, trying to stop the fighting.

Lysette laughed nastily. "We already know that ***his*** life is more important than yours. After all this time, I never thought you'd choose emotion over magic."

"You heartless … you'll never understand humans or their emotions…"

"I find it funny that you've become so righteous about humans and their emotions!"

"Don't!" Aurora warned, her hair turning purple. The talisman around her neck had started to create a soft glow. "Do ***not*** go there!"

"Seems to me that only ten years ago…"

"Stop!" Aurora demanded, power emanating from her

voice as black started to ripple through her hair.

Lysette smirked in amusement. "Oh, I see. You don't want your little hero to know about your past indiscretions. Are you fearful that he won't trust you anymore?"

"Enough!" Christopher bellowed, surprising the other occupants of the room. He crossed the room in three strides, grabbed Aurora by her upper arms, and drew her in close; keeping her nose only inches from his. "It's not worth it," he said, his commanding whisper resonating in her ears.

She let out her breath in a forced huff and looked him straight in the eyes. "She makes me…!"

"I know." His voice was soothing, trying desperately to smooth the feathers Lysette had ruffled.

"She was going to…!"

He nodded. "I know … and I don't care."

"She does it on purpose!"

Christopher allowed a small laugh to escape as he smiled in understanding. "Let it go. Whatever it is, it's not important." She tried to look around him to glare at her mentor, but he gave her a gentle shake to draw her attention back to his eyes. "We will just leave. We're done here."

Aurora sighed again, this time rolling her head from side to side, causing every vertebrae in her neck to crack as the black and purple seemed to ripple out as if she were shaking water out of her hair.

Gwenyth watched all this with apprehension, but when Aurora's hair returned to its normal shade, she breathed a sigh of relief. Lysette just watched the exchange with amusement.

Sir Christopher turned to face Lysette, releasing his partner from the grip he had used to get her back under control. "Thank you for all your help, Madam, but we feel that we have worn out our welcome. The magic is calling and we must go where it leads."

Lysette let out a curt and disapproving laugh. "Oh, who am I kidding? Go on, go save the world one monster at a time. The magic is probably drawing you to the ogre that's been terrorizing three nearby kingdoms."

Christopher sighed. "Sounds like I have a long day ahead of me."

"Watch out for each other. This is a dangerous journey ... for both of you. Here," she said, plucking a satchel out of thin air, "You might need this."

Christopher bowed and accepted it graciously, slinging it over his right shoulder. "Thank you for everything Madam. *Nur comain*, as always."

Lysette's eyes were wide in awe when she heard Christopher say thank you in Gaelic. "The man has unexpected depths," she muttered as she turned to Aurora and nodded slightly; Aurora returned the gesture before heading for the stairs that would return them to a world of men.

"A pleasure to meet you," Gwenyth murmured as she gave her best royal curtsy. "Thank you for the dress." With that, she scurried up the stairs after Aurora.

Christopher turned to follow his companions, but Lysette grabbed his right bicep in her right hand. "You take care of her, you hear me?" she hissed. His eyes went wide in disbelief as she began to dig her fingernails into his arm. "If anything happens to her, you'll have me to deal with."

He pried her fingers off his arm. "You know as well as I

that Aurora will not allow me to take care of her, but you have my word, Madam, that I would never intentionally place her in harm's way." With that, he turned and nearly ran up the stairs.

Chapter X
An Ogre Encounter

Christopher breathed a sigh of relief as he emerged into the open air of the forest. The fog seemed to be drawn back into the mystical staircase he had just exited, and as the last wisps crossed the threshold, the roots of the tree moved back into place to conceal the staircase.

"Goodbye, Lysette," Aurora whispered. "*Nur comain*." With that, she turned her back on the tree and seemed to lose herself in her thoughts as she stared at the forest.

"That was an adventure," Gwenyth ventured, shaking the dust from her pale blue skirts and then patting Jonathan on the nose. Christopher felt he could breathe again now that they were out of the sorceress' lair and he rubbed the inside of his right arm with his thumb, trying to remove the sting from her parting grip.

"What did she give us?" Gwenyth asked, still petting Jonathan.

Christopher knelt down to open the mysterious satchel, and Aurora turned to see what he would uncover.

"Let's see … food … what appears to be several bags of magic powder … an oil skin with wine in it … a rope? Hmm … why does she think we need a rope?"

Aurora knelt down next to him. "Well, she does see the future. Maybe she knows we'll need it."

"You see the future. Why don't you know we shall need it?"

Aurora scowled at him. "I only see pieces, you know that. I've never been able to see the whole future because I've never properly detached myself from the outcome of events in the present. I have not learned to let go and I care too much. That tends to get me in trouble," she said, grinning in his direction.

He just shook his head at her. "Of that I am well aware."

The princess yawned audibly, her ladylike breeding momentarily abandoned. "When are we going to rest for the night? And where?"

Aurora glanced at the sky, but the dense forest blocked out any hope of a glimpse at anything beyond. "I had completely forgotten what time of the day it was." Then, as if she were speaking to herself, "Lysette's always had a way of doing that."

Christopher raised his eyebrows quizzically, but refrained from saying anything regarding her private thoughts. "Well, why don't you figure out what kind of powders Lysette decided you would need, and then we will find a good place to spend the night." He tossed the package in her direction and she snatched it gracefully.

"Hopefully far away from here," Gwenyth muttered, shuffling her skirts nervously.

Aurora spent several quiet minutes examining the bundle of magic from Lysette, adding some of it to the powders around her waist, and tucking others into her belt to examine more closely later. When she finished, she transformed into a jaguar and began to slink off down the path.

"I guess that means we're leaving," he said with a small chuckle, slinging the bag over his shoulder as he got to his feet.

"She is not going to tell us what the powders were for?"

Gwenyth queried as she climbed onto Jonathan's back and waited for Christopher to join her.

"If I had to guess, Aurora is probably still trying to process what she received. You see, Lysette is privy to knowledge of all future events, while Aurora is privy only to some. Lysette most likely gave her each of those powders knowing why we will need them. I'm assuming it's the same with the rope. Because Aurora doesn't see the whole picture, she's probably over-analyzing all the pieces. She will tell us when she's ready, assuming she manages to decipher their uses at all." He climbed up behind the princess and clicked his tongue, signaling to Jonathan that it was time to go. The large war horse got to his feet and began trotting down the dark path after Aurora.

They finally caught up with the wayward sorceress at a small meadow only a quarter of a league ahead, but she was stopped dead in her tracks in the middle of the path, her ears pricked forward attentively, every muscle poised to strike.

"What is it?" he asked, sliding off Jonathan's back and drawing his sword as he walked up behind her. His query, however, went unacknowledged.

Her right ear twitched forward and back again, but other than that, she remained still as stone. Gwenyth glanced around nervously. The forest was no longer as dense as it had been close to Lysette's house. There was plenty of room to make a mad dash off the path if she needed Jonathan to get her out of harm's way, but she found herself desperately hoping that it wouldn't be necessary.

Aurora's ear twitched again. Christopher waited patiently, wondering silently what her cat ears had picked up that he couldn't sense.

Finally, she broke the silence. "***Something's*** coming." He glanced around for signs as to the direction danger was coming from. "Lots … of somethings," she said, amending her previous statement.

Christopher strained his ears until a dull roar could barely be heard above the noise of the forest. He could make out the sounds of rapidly squeaking wagon wheels, the pounding of running horse hooves, the panicked cries of children and the nervous lowing of domestic animals. The noises became louder and more defined, and Christopher began to glance around, trying desperately to hide his unease from the women he was trying to protect. Jonathan danced nervously from one foot to another and snorted in apprehension.

"Look out!" Aurora cried out, jumping out of the middle of the path and knocking Christopher over to get him out of harm's way. No sooner had she done so than a stampede of villagers came pouring out of the forest to their right. They had piled their meager belongings into carts pulled by panicked horses; cows and goats were tied behind while the villagers ran alongside with children or bundles clutched to their chests and torches grasped in their hands.

"Run for your lives! This place is cursed!" several cried out.

Then, as quickly as the villagers had come upon them, they were gone. Aurora picked her feline body up out of the dirt and shook herself off, morphing into huntress form and standing up. Christopher groaned and rolled over.

"He landed on his sword!" Gwenyth cried in panic.

"No … I'm good," he groaned. "I missed the dangerous end."

Aurora shook her head at him and offered him her hand to help him up. "Well, I'd wager we've found the ogre."

He stood up and dusted himself off. "I believe in this case that I would be a fool to wager against you." He glanced to the right as he picked up his sword. "Shall we?"

The small band of travelers turned off the path and headed into the forest, traveling in the opposite direction the villagers had been. Less than twenty paces later, the trees simply stopped. Stretching out in every direction before them was flat farmland. There was not a tree in sight until the other end of the valley.

Aurora turned her head from side to side, slowly taking in this new development. "Somebody had fun," she said sarcastically.

Not four paces in front of them was a broken wagon, pitched into the dirt at an awkward angle because of the broken axle. The crops beyond had been trampled by feet that left a footprint the length of Christopher's arm from fingertips to shoulder. The nearest building was still smoldering, even though the fire that had devoured its insides had gone out, but it was clear that many of the other farms were still on fire.

"An ogre," Christopher muttered. "Why couldn't it be something easy … like a griffin?"

"No one ever said this job would be easy. So, are we ready to try defeating this unwanted guest?"

"If you have any ideas, please let me know."

"You mean you do not have a plan?!" Gwenyth exclaimed.

"Are you kidding? We're making this up as we go!" Aurora turned back to Christopher. "Anything?"

He shook his head. "Maybe if we had some rope, I might be able to come up with something…"

Aurora glared at no one in particular. "We do … thanks to Lysette."

"Oh, I forgot about that. You know, it would be really annoying when she does that if it wasn't so helpful." He turned to one of Jonathan's many saddle bags and finished removing his armor. Gwenyth climbed down from Jonathan's back and crossed her arms impatiently.

"Well, why are you not rushing off to face almost certain death in order to save the day?!" she demanded.

He shot her an incredulous look. "Are you really trying to tell me how to do my job?"

The princess adopted a pouty look. "The knights of my mother's kingdom would not have been standing around ***discussing*** how to proceed; they would have already done something."

"Well, with that great plan of attack, I can't fathom why they failed to rescue you and we succeeded," Aurora smirked at her from under her dark impish lashes.

Gwenyth simply glared back haughtily, choosing to ignore the statement and turning her back on the impertinent sorceress. "Have you come up with a suitable plan of attack?" she asked.

Christopher glanced past her to meet his partner's gaze, hoping she had come up with a better plan than he had. Aurora raised her eyebrows and shrugged her shoulders. "We could always…" he said hopefully.

Aurora shook her head. "Sunrise is still a few hours off. What about…?" she trailed off, glancing from the rope in his hands to Jonathan, who was waiting patiently for them to make a decision.

He shook his head. "We would need another horse … unless…"

Aurora glared at him. "Nope, sorry, ain't gonna happen. Nobody's riding me. Not even you, Hero."

"Well, then…" he trailed off as he met Aurora's eyes. As if one, they turned to look at Gwenyth.

"What?" she demanded. "Is there something in my hair?"

Aurora grinned devilishly, "Ogres … have a thing for princesses."

Gwenyth crossed her arms. "I beg your pardon?"

Aurora chuckled nervously. "They love the taste of royal blood."

The princess threw up her arms in protest. "Oh no! I refuse to be bait for that … monster! You cannot make me!"

"Oh, come on. It's not like we're going to let anything happen to you. Aurora will use magic to protect you and I will be there to catch the ogre before anything happens."

"That is not very reassuring." She hesitated. "You are certain you cannot do this without me?" she finally asked.

Christopher and Aurora looked at each other and shrugged. "Of course not!" they said together. The princess thankfully missed the fake sincerity in their tone.

"Very well, I will consent to this madness, but only if you both take note that I was against this from the start."

"We'll try to remember that," Aurora said with a hint of sarcasm. She began rubbing her hands together in preparation. "Okay, so what's the plan?"

"Well, I was thinking that I could sneak through the forest at the other end of the valley and come up behind the ogre. Hopefully, he's asleep by now and he won't hear me coming. We can have Gwenyth ride Jonathan into the clearing, scream to attract his attention, and as he's trying to catch her, we," he said, grinning and holding up the rope from Lysette, "can catch him."

"Then what?" Gwenyth demanded.

"What do you mean, 'then what'? We'll have him trapped." Christopher looked to Aurora for help.

Gwenyth scoffed. "That does not exactly sound like a flawless plan. What if you ***do not*** manage to capture him in time? If he eats me…"

"You'll what?!" Aurora snarled, her body morphing back into the black jungle cat, her tail swishing in anticipation.

Gwenyth swallowed her empty threat and looked off into the distance, fear and dread showing plain on her face. Jonathan came up behind her and nuzzled her shoulder in support.

"Ladies … play nice. It's going to take all three of us…" Jonathan snorted at his deficient math. "Sorry, four of us to defeat the ogre."

Gwenyth sighed in defeat and nodded to Jonathan, who gingerly dropped to his knees to allow her to once again scramble up into the saddle. Christopher leapt nimbly into the saddle behind her and the great horse got to his feet. Aurora seemed to disappear into the darkness, presumably to go locate the ogre and come back with the best way to proceed.

The adventurers reached the edge of the forest at the opposite end of the farmland and began slowly working their way along the tree line. After a lengthy amount of time passed in silence, Christopher reined in his horse and slowly slid down his left flank to the ground.

Gwenyth glanced around nervously. Sunrise was still three hours away and the perpetual darkness was beginning to play tricks on her eyes. A shadow in the trees moved and she had to stifle a scream when the shadow developed glowing orbs that seemed to look right through her.

"The ogre is just ahead, around this next outcropping of trees," Aurora, still in cat form, whispered, the glowing orbs blinking at the princess. "The breeze is blowing from the north-west."

"Good. I can surprise him. Be safe, Princess. Just distract him long enough that I can sneak up on him. If he's asleep, don't scream. We will just tie him up."

"If the rope will even hold him," Gwenyth muttered dejectedly.

Christopher flashed her a reassuring smile and then darted into the trees, moving soundlessly, free from the constriction of armor. Aurora smiled slyly, her feline incisors gleaming in the soft light of the moon. "Don't forget to scream." She leapt to a nearby tree branch and faded back into the shadows.

Gwenyth took a deep breath to steady her nerves. "You know, I am not quite sure what scares me more: Aurora or the ogre." Jonathan nickered softly in agreement. She patted his neck and leaned forward. "Okay, boy, shall we go create a distraction?" The horse snorted, pawed at the ground and then trotted off in the direction Aurora had told them to look for trouble.

Christopher managed to slink through the forest, coming up behind, and downwind of, the resting ogre. To Christopher's dismay, however, the ogre wasn't asleep; he was leaned against a tree, picking his teeth with a discarded animal bone. Christopher silently climbed one of the nearby trees with overhanging branches and began working the rope into a lasso with which to snare the ogre. He glanced around in apprehension, searching for the moving shadow that would give away Aurora's position at this pre-dawn hour. Her cat-eyes gleamed at him from the darkness and that was enough to settle his nerves as he waited for Gwenyth to appear.

The ogre sat up in anticipation when a slight breeze alerted him to the approach of a royal snack. "Here we go," Christopher whispered, and Aurora swished her tail in anticipation.

The princess and the proud warhorse entered the clearing tentatively, unsure what direction the attack would come from. The ogre cumbersomely got to his feet and Gwenyth let out her shrill scream of terror at the first sight of him. He stood nearly fifteen feet tall, his scraggly hair hanging in dirty clumps from his grimy scalp. His clothes, such as they were, were stained with the dried blood of any villagers and their livestock that had failed to get away from his grubby, greedy fingers.

Christopher inched along the branch, trying desperately to get a good shot with the rope. Gwenyth screamed again and Jonathan reared in panic.

"She's a good actress," Aurora commented. "I wasn't sure she could do it."

Christopher crept down the branch to throw his lasso. "I'm not sure she's acting. We better catch this thing before she passes out and gets eaten."

Aurora looked at him in disbelief. "You mean … that wasn't part of the plan?"

He glared at her, turned, leaned and threw the lasso.

Unfortunately, the ogre had heard them. He side-stepped Christopher's lasso, turned and grabbed the rope, yanking Christopher right out of the tree.

"Chris!" Aurora shrieked, morphing back into human form and reaching a hand out to grab him, but she wasn't fast enough.

He landed with a thud, flat on his back and let go of the rope. Jonathan came galloping to the rescue, bringing the screaming Gwenyth along for the ride. The ogre swung back around, his long arms nearly connecting with Jonathan's face as the war horse suddenly reared up to protect his master. Christopher tried to scramble out of the way, but the hideous ogre managed to grab his right leg and hoist him in the air.

"Aurora!" he yelled as his world turned upside-down. "Do something!"

The ogre had picked up a rock and it looked like he was going to swing his hands together and crush Christopher's skull with the rock. Jonathan, sensing his master's peril, reared up defensively, throwing Gwenyth to the ground in the process. Her shrill scream echoed in the ogre's unprotected ears until unconsciousness claimed the princess, but not before the ogre dropped the rock in his confusion.

Aurora attempted to distract the ogre with some impromptu magic, but to no avail. He reached down and swatted at Jonathan, causing the large horse to dash out of the way. Then, he wrapped his left hand around Gwenyth's tiny waist and hoisted her into the air as well.

"Aurora!" Christopher hollered again, managing to unsheathe his sword to try to swing at the ogre's wrist.

Aurora began casting every protection spell she could

think of in her panicked state, completely unaware that her emotions were causing the gentle green glow of the talisman to begin pulsating with power. She watched Gwenyth's head loll to one side like a rag doll and she glanced desperately at Jonathan. She was quickly running out of options.

"Do something!" Christopher yelled again, taking another swing at the ogre with his sword.

Aurora had, by this time, managed to climb down from the safety of her tree and she was attempting to sneak up on the ogre. He swung around and bared his teeth, his guttural growl blowing the stench of rotted flesh in her face.

"Ugh!" she exclaimed, scurrying back to the safety of the tree line. "What am I supposed to do? It's like he has eyes in the back of his head!"

The ogre let out a terrible howl and dropped Christopher on his head. Aurora screamed in panic as the knight barely managed to roll out of the way to keep from getting stepped on.

"Blind him! I don't know!" Christopher cried out, swinging his sword at the ogre's ankle as it tried to step on him again. "Just do something!"

Aurora glanced up at their adversary and was horrified to discover that he ***was*** in possession of two sets of eyes: one in front, and one in back. "How am I supposed to get close enough to blind him when he can see in every direction at once?!"

The ogre howled in confusion, and this time, both travelers saw the flash of green light as the ogre sprouted more eyes all over his head.

"Oops! Aurora cried out, clasping her hands over her mouth.

"Aurora! The talisman!" Christopher bellowed, scrambling out from underfoot as the ogre became confused and began stumbling around. "You have to get back in control!" He managed to make it to the tree line and hide, gasping for breath. "Stop thinking with your emotions!"

"You sound like Lysette!" she hollered back, her hair shifting back and forth between orange and purple. "How am I supposed to keep my emotions in check while you're nearly getting stomped on by the blob of eyeballs?!"

The flash of bright green light caught her off guard and she threw up her hands to shield her eyes. Christopher watched in slow motion as the ogre began sprouting eyeballs all over his body. His legs could no longer hold his weight, so they collapsed beneath him, bringing his bulk down to the ground. He continued to bellow in pain and fear as his midsection, with nothing to support it, also succumbed to gravity. Willing to risk the possibility of getting squished, Christopher dashed toward the wailing ogre and barely managed to break Gwenyth's fall with his body as the ogre's hand transformed and his whole arm seemed to congeal into the mound, no longer able to hold onto his prize.

Christopher stood and scooped up the unconscious princess, glaring at Aurora as she cautiously approached the towering blob that was now before them. The creature continued to wail in agony until the spell caught up with his head, silencing him with a sickening gurgle as there was nothing left but a mound of blinking eyes.

Aurora turned to Christopher guiltily, but he threw up his hand to silence her. "Don't even say it!" He glared at her as the light emanating from the talisman changed from a pulsating green light to a soft green glow. "I never thought I would say this, but Lysette is right about that thing."

She looked at him, defeat plain in her eyes. "I know."

Christopher knelt down and began trying to revive the princess, while Aurora went back to pacing around the mound of eyeballs the size of a haystack.

"This was completely unintentional."

Christopher glared at her. "You have to keep a level head. That's the only way this works," he said, gesturing back and forth between them, "if you keep a level head and ***I*** panic." She laughed a little at the way he used logic to cheer her up. "You know full well that if we both panic, chaos ensues. Leave the panicking to me … I'm better at it."

She laughed again and shook her head. "The only problem with that being even when you're panicked, you're more level-headed than I am."

Christopher didn't have a chance to respond because Gwenyth began to stir. Her eyes fluttered open and she asked in a weak voice, "Did we get him?"

"In a manner of speaking," Christopher said with a smirk.

Aurora pulled the wineskin provided by Lysette from the satchel and added a small pinch of purple powder to it. "Drink some of this," she commanded Gwenyth, who was too dazed to argue.

"What's that for?" Christopher asked.

"To stave off a concussion." His blank look caused her to roll her eyes. "She bumped her head. I'm just trying to make sure she's alright."

As her vision cleared, Gwenyth found she was unable to focus on Christopher's face. The only thing she could see was the mound of eyes blinking at her in unison. "That is hideous," she gasped as Christopher helped her to her feet.

"Yeah," he agreed, "but at least he won't be terrorizing any more villagers."

Gwenyth's face took on a slightly green hue as she continued to stare at the eyes. "I think I am going to be ill," she said, both hands flying up to cover her mouth.

"What do we do with it?" he asked, cocking his head and looking at the eyeball mound as if it were nothing more than an inconvenient piece of landscape.

"We could set him on fire," Aurora suggested.

He shook his head in disbelief. "Not feeling very merciful today, are we?" His eyebrows were raised in a gesture meant to chastise her.

Aurora scowled in his direction. "Lysette … being right…" she trailed off.

Christopher nodded his head in understanding. He imagined it wasn't easy being reminded you're nothing more than a novice.

Gwenyth inhaled sharply. "Whatever we are going to do with it, can we do it soon? I do not know what is worse … the sight of it or the smell of it!"

Aurora glanced at each of her companions in turn, shrugged her shoulders, and snapped her fingers. To Gwenyth's utter horror, the mass of eyeballs burst into flames.

"Aurora!" Christopher exclaimed, glaring at her.

"Oh, don't get all righteous on me. What were we going to do with him if we tied him up? It's not like we would have left him alive!" Her scarlet hair became shorter and darker as she morphed into the jungle cat. "Come on, Hero. Let's find a suitable place for 'her highness' to sleep … before she passes out again."

Christopher turned and was barely able to reach out his arms before Gwenyth collapsed into him, fatigue, nausea and a possible concussion finally overtaking her. "Great," the valiant hero muttered as he attempted to jostle the princess into a better position so that he could scoop her into his arms and carry her. "Come on, boy," he said as he started walking away from the stench of Aurora's latest magical mishap, Jonathan plodding along behind him.

Christopher caught up with Aurora at a nearby farm that was upwind of the ogre's remains. "You can spend the night in what's left of the barn," she said. "I'll keep watch, since I can go longer without sleep than you can. Don't worry about anything … just sleep until you're both ready to travel. With any luck, Aliwyn is only a day or two away."

He sighed in defeat as he managed to throw the princess over his right shoulder and pull a blanket from Jonathan's saddle bag. He easily spread it out on what was left of a pile of hay and then gently placed the unconscious princess on top of it. He then bunked against the remains of a beam for the night.

Aurora watched him from the shadows until she was sure he was asleep and then she paced restlessly, waiting for the sun to come up.

Chapter XI
A Heroine's Welcome

The next morning, Aurora caught the scent of a royal official and his entourage of knights heading in their direction. Grinning slyly to herself, she found a spot in the barn that would place her behind them when they approached her sleeping companions. She waited patiently for the strangers to appear and her persistence paid off.

One of the knights sounded a horn as the large group approached the sleeping travelers with swords drawn. "State your names, your business in Romalia, and tell us if you have seen the terrible ogre that has been roaming the countryside."

Christopher rubbed the sleep from his eyes as he slowly measured his opponents, noticing that Gwenyth had not stirred at the sound of the horn. He searched for Aurora as he cautiously chose his words, knowing full well she must be nearby because of the way all the horses were acting except for Jonathan. "My name is Sir Christopher of Calidore, and this is Milady, the Princess Gwenyth of Aliwyn. We are simply passing through your kingdom on our way to Aliwyn, and the princess is a little worse for the wear this morning because of our encounter with the terrible beast last night."

The lord sat forward on his horse, even as the animal nervously moved about beneath him. "You have encountered the ogre and lived? Hurry, tell me everything! I must send a report to his grace about what it will take to defeat the creature!"

Christopher's eyes went wide and he laughed, causing the lord to become angry. "I wish to know what it is that you find so amusing, young man!" he demanded.

Aurora chose that moment to slink out of the shadows behind them, spooking all the horses as she passed. "He's laughing because you're about four hours too late." She curled up next to Sir Christopher, her large yellow eyes measuring the arrivals hungrily. The one in the back tried to reach a bow and arrow without attracting attention to himself. "Try it and lose an arm!" she growled, her tail swishing in anticipation of the pounce.

"Aurora, behave," Christopher said, hoping she was still in control of her animal instincts.

"I find it quite untenable that you, the cat, and the princess succeeded where whole armies have failed."

Christopher shrugged, quite used to the incredulous reactions he had been getting since he met the princess. He then turned to the knights. "Gentlemen, I would suggest you keep your hands in plain sight and don't make any sudden movements. Aurora has been in animal form so much the last few days that I'm not sure she will be able to resist her basic animal instincts. I'm going to see if I can revive the princess. Since you won't take my word for it, perhaps because she is of royal blood, you will believe her." He was simply too worn out to argue any further on his behalf.

The lord looked down at Christopher in disdain, almost as if he wanted to challenge Christopher's right to call himself a knight, but Aurora inched forward into a better pouncing position, and he quickly decided it was prudent to remain silent. "It's your move, darlin'," she growled with a hungry grin. The lord simply gulped visibly as he stared at her gleaming feline incisors.

"Princess? Milady, you need to wake up. Can you hear me?"

After several tense moments, the princess finally stirred. Her eyes fluttered open and her complexion just seemed to glow as Christopher helped her to her feet. Even her hair appeared to be a brighter spun-gold color than usual, and the pale blue dress sparkled in the early morning sunlight.

"Where am I? What has happened? Where is the hideous creature?"

Christopher struggled to hide his grin. "Gone, Milady. Don't you remember?"

"How silly of me. I must have hit my head. Did we win? Have I been asleep long?"

He shook his head. "Yes, we won and you have been asleep for four hours."

"Oh, dear." She glanced around and noticed the lord and his knights for the first time. "Really, all this fuss just because we defeated an ogre." She attempted to smooth her hair and skirt. "Sir Christopher, you never told me that we would receive a hero's welcome!" Her sickly sweet princess voice and her sparkling gown began to charm the newcomers, while it left Christopher and Aurora staring at each other in disbelief.

"Milady, am I to understand that the … ***three*** of you defeated the ogre not four hours ago?"

She smiled and batted her eyes at him. "Actually, the four of us defeated the ogre. Jonathan played his part well." At the princess' praise, the great steed pawed the ground and tossed his mane proudly.

"And where did this fight take place?" the lord queried, giving Jonathan a sidelong glance.

"Sir Christopher, where were we last night?"

He shook his head in disbelief before he answered. "Several minutes ride to the southeast, right at the edge of the forest."

The lord nodded his head and two of his knights reined in their horses and went to investigate the battleground. "Milady, it sounds as if you have had a very trying ordeal and I would be honored if you would allow me to escort you to Castle Treconia. In fact, you may ride with me," he said, reaching down and offering her his hand.

Christopher stiffened at this obvious snub from the lord, turning to pick up the forgotten blanket Gwenyth had slept on as he listened to the lord try to charm Gwenyth. He quickly shook the plain piece of cloth to remove the pieces of hay, but as he went to shove it in the saddle bag, Jonathan let out a dismayed whinny. He trotted over and knelt before the princess, practically begging her to ride him.

She laughed gaily and patted Jonathan on the neck before she looked up at the lord and smiled sweetly. "Milord, I will gladly accept your offer of an escort, but I am afraid I must decline the ride. This noble steed has been instrumental in keeping me alive and I dare not insult his pride. Sir Christopher, if you please?"

Christopher couldn't help but grin triumphantly as he finally managed to put the blanket away and then wrapped his hands around her tiny waist and lifted her easily onto Jonathan's saddle.

The lord eyed Aurora suspiciously. "We keep a swift pace on these horses. Can the cat keep up?"

"She will manage," Christopher said.

"Manage?" Aurora scoffed as she began running, took a flying leap, and in midair, morphed into her hawk form. Christopher barely had time to lift his right arm so that she could land gracefully on it like a perch. "Don't worry about me, boys. I'll ***manage***," she said, clicking her beak for emphasis.

Christopher shook his head. "Show-off," he muttered before turning to the entourage that was now staring at them with mouths agape and grinned broadly for show.

"You did offer us an escort, did you not?" the princess interrupted sweetly.

The lord finally found his tongue and turned his attention back to the princess. "Yes, of course. Whenever you are ready, Milady."

She smiled. "Sir Christopher?"

With one smooth motion, he launched himself into the saddle behind Gwenyth, barely ruffling Aurora's red-gold feathers as she went along for the ride. He reached around Gwenyth with his left hand and gathered the reins, clicking his tongue to signal Jonathan to get to his feet. "Ready," he finally replied.

"Lead the way, Milord," Gwenyth commanded, still smiling sweetly.

The lord bowed and turned his entourage away from the barn, his six remaining knights taking up flanking positions around the weary travelers.

The lord immediately engaged Gwenyth in conversation, extracting details from her about their encounter with the ogre, leaving Christopher and Aurora to their thoughts. As they neared Castle Treconia, they began to get an accurate assessment of the damage to the kingdom. Even close to the castle walls, the ogre had decimated the farmland. Keeping her voice at a whisper so that even Gwenyth couldn't hear her, Aurora turned to Christopher, "These poor people. It will be years before the land has healed itself enough that they can farm again." She turned her head, her hawk eyes able to see much farther than his.

"Is there anything you can do for them?" he asked, matching her whispered tones.

She tilted her head. "You mean, with magic? I'd have to think about that."

"Speaking of magic, are you responsible for the magical glow that has been radiating off Gwenyth?"

Aurora scoffed. "No. If I had to guess, I'd say that glow is courtesy of Lysette's gown."

Christopher nodded. "She ***was*** awfully insistent that Gwenyth have a new dress."

"I swear that woman lives to drive me crazy!"

Christopher chuckled, but otherwise held his tongue. He knew better than to provoke another argument about Lysette. Thankfully, they were crossing the castle's drawbridge by this time and they didn't have a chance to finish their conversation.

"Make way! Make way for the saviors of Romalia! Make way!" the herald, one of their retinue, cried out.

Christopher squirmed in the saddle, extremely uncomfortable with receiving a hero's welcome. Aurora, still perched on his arm, simply examined everything with a lofty air, as if it was their due; Gwenyth waved and smiled graciously at everyone they passed. The herald sounded the horn as they reached the castle's inner gate, and the doors were opened for a man who appeared to be only about ten years Christopher's senior. His regal attire was unbuttoned and unkempt, as if he had dressed in a hurry. "What is it? Is the castle under attack? Where is the ogre?"

Gwenyth giggled playfully. "I am sorry to disappoint you, but all this fuss is for us. I am afraid we took care of your ogre problem last night."

The newcomer blinked twice and then stepped forward to help her down from the horse. "I am William III, Duke of Romalia, and I believe, gracious lady, that I am in your debt."

Chapter XII
Love at First Sight

After a quick round of introductions, the duke led his guests into the castle, raving about how brave and brilliant the tired travelers were. Aurora, still in hawk form, kept glancing around for rodents to chase, hoping for some distraction from the incessant prattle of the nobility. The duke kept stopping anyone they passed in the halls and had Gwenyth repeat the tale of the ogre's defeat. Christopher followed in silence, always three steps behind, perfectly content to allow the loquacious princess to be the center of attention.

"The way she's going on, you'd think she had dispatched the ogre all by herself," Aurora muttered, snapping her beak closed curtly.

Christopher turned and grinned at her. "Why, didn't you know? It was ***she*** who rescued ***us*** from the foul creature!" With that, the two of them burst out laughing, drawing the attention of the royals.

"Oh, are you two still here?" Gwenyth mused. "I thought you would have been resting up in your quarters by now."

"Oh, how inhospitable of me! You must be exhausted after all your travels." The duke waved his hand and a servant approached cautiously.

"If you would like, I can take your bird to the aviary," the servant said quietly. "Then I can take you to your quarters."

Aurora clicked her beak in annoyance, but elected not to

speak. Christopher swallowed his urge to laugh at the idiocy of his comment and glanced at Gwenyth. For once, the princess got the hint. "Oh, no. ***She*** is a special bird. Arrange for her to have quarters next to his."

The duke raised his eyebrows skeptically, but nodded his consent to the page, who proceeded to lead Christopher and Aurora off down the hall.

"The aviary," Aurora scoffed, keeping her voice low enough that the page couldn't hear. "As if I'm just some ordinary bird. Does this look like the plumage of an ordinary bird?"

Christopher stifled a laugh as they followed the page up a stairwell. "No. I will admit, I have always thought you had the coloring of a phoenix rather than a hawk," he whispered.

She turned her head and looked at her brilliant blood red and glistening gold feathers. "Phoenix, huh? I like the sound of that."

The page cleared his throat, drawing their attention. "Your chambers. An attendant will arrive at sundown with formal-wear for dinner in the banquet hall. You may rest until then." With a stiff bow, he turned and left.

Christopher opened the first door and peeked into the room. It was simply furnished: a bear rug on the floor, a four-poster bed, a blazing fire, a wardrobe, and an end-table with a lit candle and a wash basin. He walked into the room and closed the door so that Aurora could transform without startling the servants.

She flapped her wings, and in mid-flight she morphed back to human form, landing in a crouching position on the rug. "Not bad," she commented, standing up and looking around.

"I'm across the hall," he said, indicating absently with his thumb. "I'm exhausted, so I'm going to get some rest. I will see you at dinner." He walked to the door and as he opened it, he turned back to face her. "Holler if you need me."

She laughed. "That's normally my line."

He just grinned and left the room. She watched him shut the door behind him before she collapsed on the bed out of sheer exhaustion. She was his protector, and as such she would brave any trials and endure a myriad of abuses in order to keep him safe without ever letting him know how it affected her.

"I think I aged a hundred years in the last fortnight," she said to no one in particular, staring up at the ceiling. Though she'd never admit it, the string of adventures they'd had since rescuing Gwenyth had stretched her nearly to the breaking point, and now it was time for some well deserved rest. With a heavy sigh, she curled up on her side and fell asleep.

Christopher couldn't believe how tired he was. His head still ached where the ogre had dropped him on it, and he couldn't remember the last time his body didn't hurt. He went to the wash basin on the end-table and tried to clean some of the grime off his face.

As an after thought, he removed his travel-soiled tunic and examined the arrow wound in his shoulder. Thanks to Aurora's magic, it had healed quickly, but as always, it had left an angry looking scar where the arrowhead had gone straight through.

He sighed. His torso was covered in scars that never seemed to fade from wounds Aurora had had to use magic to heal in a hurry. "I swear, I think I've aged a hundred years since we met." He pulled the covers back from the bed and crawled in, curling up and immediately falling asleep.

Hours later, as promised, servants arrived to help them

prepare for dinner. If the servants were surprised to find a woman in the quarters prepared for the bird, they did a very good job of hiding their feelings. The servants gave them the opportunity to bathe and brought them fresh garments. They dressed Aurora in a dark green brocade gown and brushed her curly red hair until it gleamed. The color of the fabric brought out her eyes with a fierce new intensity and contrasted beautifully with the blood red color of her hair. As she examined herself in the looking glass, she was amazed at how different she looked, and she laughed when she thought about how Christopher would react at the sight of her.

The servants brought Christopher a tunic made of the same dark green fabric and a pair of pants that were as black as his hair. His normally unkempt hair was actually combed, but it could never be tamed. He strapped on his sword belt, more out of habit than anything else, and stepped out into the hall.

Aurora was waiting in the hall, a demure smile on her face and Christopher let out a low whistle. "That good?" she asked, turning to show him the whole package.

"Better," he said with a grin. "I had forgotten you look like this under all that travel dust."

She smiled. "You look pretty good yourself. Shall we?" she said, glancing down the hall.

He offered her his arm and they started off, looking like they belonged at court for the first time since King Lionel fell.

The servants opened the ornate doors into the grand dining hall, and the two travelers were caught in a sea of memories. They both drifted back to the day they met in Lionel's hall. Christopher had just returned the princess and he stood looking so small amidst the royalty in the audience hall.

Aurora laughed. "You've got the same wide-eyed lost look on your face."

He looked at her in surprise. "You're thinking of that day too?"

She raised her eyebrows at him playfully. "I don't need magic to read your thoughts. Your face reads like a book."

He snorted in annoyance. "You can get all dressed up, but you're still the same old Aurora."

"You know you'd never change me. It would drain all the fun out of our relationship."

The duke was leading Gwenyth around the dining hall on his arm as if they had been friends for years. Christopher and Aurora fell in step behind them and were surprised to discover they were still talking about Gwenyth's encounter with the ogre.

"How very brave you are to have volunteered to be bait for the terrible monster," the duke was saying, patting Gwenyth's hand in tenderness.

Christopher and Aurora glanced at each other in surprise.

"Oh, it was nothing," she said, smiling at him graciously. "Christopher needed someone to distract the ogre for him, and since ogres are exceedingly fond of princesses, I knew it had to be me."

Aurora scoffed audibly and Gwenyth seemed to notice them for the first time. "Oh, Liam, you remember Sir Christopher of Calidore and the sorceress, Aurora of Beldain. They arrived with me this morning."

"I like that! We arrived with her indeed!" she protested under her breath.

"Ah, Sorceress. How nice to finally meet you in your proper form," the duke bowed, the picture of civility.

"Thank you, Milord. And my apologies for the masquerade earlier, but I find the common folk tend to panic if I perform too much magic in their presence."

He smiled. "The lower nobility tend to panic as well. Lord Allain told me of your little trick this morning."

Aurora chewed on her upper lip in embarrassment. "I'm sorry for that. I have a tendency to be rather rambunctious when I've been in cat form too long. He's actually lucky that was all I did."

"No apologies necessary. It was nice to see Lord Allain rattled. And Sir Christopher, looking much more alert."

"Yes, Milord," he said, inclining his head in a stiff bow.

"Well, you must be famished. Please be seated and I will have food brought at once."

Christopher led Aurora to a seat at the grand dining table, tucked her carved chair under the table for her, and then seated himself on her left at the end of the table so as to avoid bumping elbows with anyone. Their host seated Gwenyth across from Christopher and took the head of the table for himself. As he sat down, he banged his metal goblet on the stone table three times. The dining hall doors opened and the rest of the table's occupants flooded into the room, seating themselves wherever they could. Christopher and Aurora glanced at the new faces in surprise because the nobility and the peasants were mixed and all gathered together. They seated themselves around the table, paying no attention to the separation of class that was usually observed at royal tables. A farmer sat next to Gwenyth, and Christopher watched as a horrified gasp escaped her mouth and she visibly moved her chair away from the newcomer. A young seamstress sat next to Aurora and smiled shyly.

Aurora looked at Christopher in surprise, not because she felt the same way Gwenyth did about a commoner daring to sit next to her, but because their host actually allowed commoners to mingle with upper nobility at his royal banquet table.

"My friends," the duke said loudly, standing up to address the whole table. "The ogre has done considerable damage to all our livelihoods that I was unable to prevent. He destroyed homes, farms, crops and livestock, and I was powerless to stop it. He destroyed every army I could muster. It was only when these three travelers appeared that his reign of terror ended. These three wonderful people arrived in our darkest hour and defeated this monster that has been plaguing us. A toast to our saviors!"

A cheer of "hear, hear!" went up round the table, causing Gwenyth to blush and smile shyly, Christopher to slide down in his chair uncomfortably, and Aurora to glance around the table in silent scrutiny, a small smile appearing in one corner of her mouth.

Dinner was served with another bang of the goblet, and Aurora and Christopher were shocked at the meager banquet that was provided. "I knew that the ogre had decimated the farmland, but..." Aurora trailed off.

Gwenyth leaned over to whisper to their host, "Liam, who are all these people?"

Aurora couldn't help herself; she leaned closer to Christopher so she could hear the duke's answer.

"If you wanted to sit in my lap, all you had to do was ask," he joked in her ear as she started to lean past him.

She gripped his right thigh in her left hand and dug her fingernails in, causing him to wince. "Shh!" she commanded.

The duke was smiling and patting Gwenyth's hand. "I know they are common, but their homes were completely destroyed. They are my subjects and they had nowhere else to go. I allowed anyone who was fleeing from the ogre to move into the castle and I have been trying to provide for them ever since. As you can see," he said, gesturing to the rather pathetic banquet set before them, "my resources have been stretched rather thin."

Gwenyth glanced around, her face now showing sorrow and pity instead of disdain. "I wish there was something more we could do."

Christopher risked a sidelong glance at Aurora and tilted his head questioningly. "Oh, all right," she hissed, standing up from the table. "I'll be right back." He smiled as he watched her retreating form cross the room.

She walked through the far doorway, on the heels of one of the servants that had been serving them and followed him into the kitchen. The kitchen staff gasped, stared at her wide-eyed and huddled together, unaccustomed to seeing royal guests in their midst.

Aurora looked around, searching for the next course, and saw nothing else prepared, not even enough for the servants. She addressed the head cook. "Where is the next course?"

The cook curtseyed. "If you please, Milady, that is all we have."

Aurora looked at their hungry faces. "What about your dinners? Are you telling me that you've served everything, not even enough to feed everyone out there, and you have nothing left for yourselves?"

A young kitchen maid, no more than ten years old, stepped

forward bravely. "You are the sorceress, aren't you? Are you going to make food?"

Aurora smiled gently at the innocent face and leaned down, cupping the child's chin in her right hand. "What would you like to see in the second course?" she asked with a wink, rolling up her sleeves. The kitchen maid's face lit up as if she had scores of ideas and another servant stepped forward to tie Aurora's loose curls in a knot behind her head. "Now, who has some ideas for what we should serve?"

The duke was conversing with Gwenyth in whispered tones, and he hadn't even served himself yet. Christopher, knowing others were hungrier than he, had also refrained from serving himself, and he kept glancing at the door Aurora had gone through. He could see flickering colored lights through the crack under the door, letting him know that Aurora was indeed hard at work, but he had no idea what to expect.

The duke stood up to address the table just as Aurora walked back into the room shaking the knot out of her hair and rolling down her sleeves as she crossed to her seat.

"Now that we have all eaten our fill…" the duke was saying, even though it was obvious that no one had.

"Excuse me, Milord, but the servants have a surprise," she said with a smile, brushing a spot of flour off her shoulder.

He raised his eyebrows and readdressed the table. "As it turns out, my servants have a surprise for us." With that, he banged his goblet on the stone table and sat down again.

The servants began filing in, carrying heaping platter after platter. Pheasant, boar, deer, exotic fruit, nuts, bread, and wine filed into the room. A huge grin spread across Christopher's face as he looked over at his partner.

"Oh, quit making that ridiculous face. You know I wasn't about to let these poor people starve. The servants hadn't even saved any food for themselves."

As one of the servants filled his goblet to the brim with wine, the duke looked over at Aurora. "You are an extraordinary woman. I find myself once again in your debt."

Gwenyth coughed, slightly caught off-guard, as a few streaks of blonde shot through Aurora's hair before swiftly returning to its normal blood red color. The conversation round the table grew loud and boisterous as the subjects of Romalia were able to eat until their stomachs were full for the first time in a long time. The servants had even brought out a dessert course, to the delight of all the peasants.

To show his appreciation for defeating the ogre, creating the banquet and enlivening the spirits of his subjects, the duke decided to honor his guests with an evening of dancing. Most of the peasants were so full and tired that they scurried off to sleep, but some of the middle class joined the duke and his guests in the ballroom. As the music started, the duke whirled Gwenyth across the floor, leaving Christopher and Aurora giggling in the doorway.

"You know, I think he likes her," Christopher said, extending his hand in an invitation.

Aurora slid into his arms and they waltzed across the floor. "I don't imagine there are many men who would be able to resist her charms, especially since she's a princess."

He laughed. "She certainly has been laying on the charm since she woke up this morning."

A cloud seemed to cross Aurora's face. "I wonder if Lysette had something to do with that."

He gave her a disapproving glare. "She was your mentor … and your friend."

"Your point being?"

"Well, you always blame her for things that go wrong in our lives. Why do you hate her so much?"

Aurora sighed. "I don't hate her. She just makes learning lessons a painful experience, and she never lets you forget your mistakes, especially the big ones."

"Is one of your big mistakes whatever it was you were fighting about at her house?"

Aurora took a slow controlled breath. "Yes, but that's a story for another day."

He nodded. He knew better than to push her about her past, especially since so much of it was painful for her. He looked over at Gwenyth. "Do you think she likes him?" he asked.

Aurora shrugged. "I've seen stranger ***arranged*** marriages that worked out fine. Who knows? Maybe she sees an advantage in the match."

"Marriage?" Christopher protested a little too loudly.

"Splendid!" the duke exclaimed enthusiastically. "When will the blessed event be?"

Aurora's eyes went wide in surprise and Christopher looked at him in confusion. "Whatever do you mean?" he asked.

The duke tilted his head slightly to the side. "When will it be? I would be honored to attend your wedding."

"Our wedding?" Christopher sputtered, turning a brilliant shade of scarlet and Aurora couldn't help but smile to herself.

Thankfully, Gwenyth saved them. "Oh, they are not getting married. Their lives are rather complicated, so they do not have time for romance."

The duke inclined his head slightly in a bow. "My apologies. I heard the word marriage and I assumed you were speaking of yours."

"Actually, we were discussing ***yours***," Aurora said with a snap, discouraging any further conversation and causing both Gwenyth and the duke to look away in embarrassment. Even the musicians had stopped playing. The duke quickly tried to compose himself and waved them to continue playing.

"Nice job," Christopher whispered. "You managed to shroud the entire room in an uncomfortable silence." Aurora simply smiled.

The evening dragged on and Christopher continued watching the princess with their host, chewing on what she had said until it turned sour in his mouth.

"Quit scowling," Aurora said, interrupting his thoughts.

His eyes lost their faraway look as he slowly met her gaze. "I was just thinking about what she said."

"The 'no time for romance' comment?" She laughed at his frustrated look.

"Stay out of my head."

"I don't have to be in your head to know what you are dwelling on. I know you better than you think I do."

"I am beginning to realize that."

"Don't get so stressed about it. When you decide you want romance, you'll find a way to make time for it."

He gave her a look of suspicious confusion. "I will never understand you." She just gave him a sly, devious smile. He turned his attention back to their host. "Do you think he will ask for her hand?"

Aurora shrugged. "Her dowry definitely wouldn't hurt his suffering royal coffers. I just wonder if her parents would consent. He *is* technically beneath her."

The duke was lost in Gwenyth's sparkling innocent eyes. She kept smiling sweetly, knowing full well that he found her irresistible and she was wondering how she could use that to her advantage. "This evening has been *so* wonderful, I wish it would never end," she sighed as he whirled her around to the end of a song.

He smiled. "It does not have to."

For effect, she put on her best princess pout. "But it must. Tomorrow we continue on to Aliwyn. My mother does not even know I have been rescued."

His eyes lit up. "Aliwyn is not even three leagues from here. I could send word to your mother that you are safe. Then you could stay a little longer."

Gwenyth smiled. She had to admit the idea had merit. The longer it took to get back into her mother's clutches, the happier she'd be. "Send this ring with your messenger," she said as she slid a rather large ring bearing her royal crest off her right hand. "She will know you speak the truth."

He waved to a page and the boy stepped forward. "Bring me writing tools," he commanded and the boy bowed and hurried from the room. When he returned, the duke quickly composed a letter and sealed it with his own crest. He handed the sealed letter and Gwenyth's ring to the page. "Give these to Jense. Have him deliver them into the hand of Queen Tamera of Aliwyn, no one else. Understand?"

The page bowed and scurried from the room.

Gwenyth smiled as she and the duke continued dancing.

"The plot thickens," Aurora grinned devilishly. Christopher simply rolled his eyes.

As their night came to a close, Christopher and Aurora climbed the stairs to their chambers, arm in arm. "It was nice to feel like we had normal lives again, even if it was just for one night."

She smiled at him. "You miss the slower pace of living at court, don't you?"

He looked at her in surprise. "Don't you?"

"On occasion, but most of the time I enjoy the solitude and the freedom of our life."

He smiled. "Freedom is not necessarily the word I would have chosen, but now that you mention it, I do, too. Goodnight, Milady," he said, bowing low and kissing her hand outside her door.

"Goodnight, Good Sir."

Christopher did not sleep soundly that night. No longer exhausted and after years of sleeping on the ground, he was unable to grow accustomed to the comfort of a bed. Gwenyth's words were also haunting him, making it difficult for his mind to settle down and allow him to sleep. *He didn't have time for romance or marriage. He had a mission, and until the curse was lifted, he had to fulfill it.* He tossed and turned over these thoughts most of the night.

Chapter XIII
Enter the Queen

The next afternoon, they decided to take a leisure day in the courtyard. Their host was attempting to teach Gwenyth about hunting and falconing, but she just kept batting her innocent blue eyes at him. For lack of other amusement, Aurora and Christopher were having an archery contest, which she was winning.

He glared at her. "You're not using magic to improve your aim, are you?"

She laughed. "I don't ***need*** magic to beat ***you***." He glared again as she hit another bulls-eye.

A rider came galloping into the courtyard and reined in his horse right in front of the duke and Gwenyth. "Milady, Milord, a response from her majesty, Queen Tamera of Aliwyn."

"Thank you, Jense," the duke said, accepting the sealed letter. He glanced at Gwenyth in apprehension. "My letter did not require a response."

She sighed. "I am not surprised that Mother was of a different opinion." She smiled weakly. "We had best see what she has to say."

The duke broke the seal and read the following letter:

My dearest daughter,

I am so glad to learn of your escape from the wizard

and your journey back to Aliwyn. While I am thrilled that you are safe, I feel rather distressed that you have accepted the hospitality of the duke without a proper chaperone. For this reason, I am leaving for Romalia and shall arrive by your side within a day of your receiving this letter. I look forward to seeing you well after all this time and to hearing the tale of your escape.

Warm Regards,
Mother

He handed the letter to Gwenyth and she quickly scanned her mother's scrawling script. "Oh, dear. I was afraid of something like this," she cried out, the defiance that Christopher and Aurora had grown accustomed to gone from her voice. They looked up in surprise and lowered their bows, watching the small scene unfolding across the courtyard.

Their host looked incredibly agitated and began pacing, "I cannot believe this! It is not as if we are alone and unsupervised and her letter calls my honor into question! Why does she feel it is necessary to make the journey? You would have returned home in two days time!"

Gwenyth smiled meekly. "She has always tried to control me. She has had my future planned out since I was born. I suspect she even had all the eligible princes try to rescue me from Varuk, but none succeeded. Only Sir Christopher and Aurora were able to defeat him."

"Technically, all we did was scare him away," Aurora whispered, she and Christopher having walked closer so they could hear what was going on.

He smiled at her. "Let her hang on to her delusions. Apparently, they're all she has left."

Gwenyth was, by this time, crying into her hands. Aurora rolled her eyes. "There'd be no better time than right now to ask her."

Their host was kneeling down in front of Gwenyth, who was seated with her face buried in her hands, weeping uncontrollably. His voice was too low for them to hear anything, but Aurora could tell by the duke's face that it wasn't going well.

"Please do not cry. You have brought such a sparkle into my life that I am unwilling to let you go. This castle has been filled with strife for so long that it has been a wonderful change having you here and I am not ready to give that up."

Gwenyth tried to smile sweetly. "My mother would never approve. She probably has some eligible prince picked out and coming with her to get me as we speak."

"I really don't like this whiny version of Gwenyth. What happened to all that sass she's been feeding everyone since we met her?"

Christopher shrugged. "I have a strong suspicion that her mother is very controlling."

"You think?!" Aurora snapped.

"If that's the case, the prospect of being reunited with this woman may be sapping whatever independent spirit she developed while with us right out of her," he responded, ignoring, as always, her modern phrases that he didn't understand.

Aurora's eyes took on a far away, thoughtful look. "I wonder…"

He gave her an accusing look. "What are you plotting?" he demanded.

"Oh, hush! If it works, it will be a good thing. Besides, what have we got to lose? Gwenyth!" she called, interrupting the latest whine. "Will you come with me? I have a matter to discuss with you. Let's leave the boys to the archery contest and go inside a moment."

Gwenyth sighed deeply, wiping away her tears as she followed Aurora into the castle.

"I hope you know what you're doing," Christopher muttered, watching the retreating forms of the tenacious sorceress and the weeping princess.

"What is the matter with you?!" Aurora demanded as soon as they were out of earshot of the men.

Gwenyth burst into very unladylike heaving sobs. "I cannot help it!"

The sorceress' eyes went wide in surprise. "I'm sorry. This just isn't like you."

"I know," she sniffled. "I got so used to making my own decisions and having my voice heard that the idea of going back to being … glorified artwork … just…" she broke down into sobs again.

"Okay, well, I think our host is trying to ask for your hand, but you keep bursting into tears."

"It would be so nice to be free from my mother's grasp, but she will never agree to a match with William! He has no money and he is beneath me!" she sobbed.

"Only you can decide if he's beneath you." Aurora smiled slyly and poured a few swallows of wine into a goblet for the distraught princess. "Besides, I might just have a solution for that." She dropped a pinch of light blue powder and a pinch of white crystalline powder into the glass and whispered a few words in Gaelic, causing the liquid to smoke and bubble. "Do you trust me?"

Gwenyth looked at her skeptically and wiped away a tear. "It seems to work for Sir Christopher, so yes."

Aurora smiled and handed the teary-eyed princess the goblet. "The whole thing," she commanded.

"But it is wine!" Gwenyth protested, wiping away another tear.

"Trust me, becoming drunk would only help at this point," she joked. When Gwenyth simply sniffled and stared at her teary-eyed, she added, "There isn't enough wine to make you drunk."

Gwenyth sighed in defeat and swallowed the strange liquid. When she brought the cup down away from her lips, there was a different gleam in her eye. She took a deep breath and the tears stopped flowing. She took another deep breath and the fire returned to her eyes, the color flowed back into her cheeks and face, and her back straightened up with royal conviction. She looked at Aurora in confusion. "We really should not have left our host like that. Did you require something?"

Aurora smiled slyly. "Nope. I did what I needed to. How are you feeling?"

Gwenyth frowned. "I do not believe breakfast is sitting well with me, but other than that, I feel fine."

The women returned to the courtyard, and as Aurora rejoined Christopher by the archery equipment, she still had a large grin on her face.

"Proud of yourself?" Christopher whispered as she slid her arm through his.

"Just watch," she replied, her green eyes sparkling with playful mischief.

"Milady, are you alright?" their host asked in concern.

"I am so sorry, William. I do not know what came over me today. You were attempting to discuss something with me before I rudely burst into tears. Please continue."

"What did you do?" Christopher hissed.

"I gave her back her spine. She's assertive again."

"The difference is not exactly subtle."

Aurora simply shrugged.

The duke looked slightly taken aback by the change in Gwenyth, but he didn't let that sap his courage. "Milady, as I was saying, you have brought life back into this kingdom. I would like very much to ask for your hand in marriage, and you would do me the greatest honor if you would accept. I know that you cannot possibly love me after only knowing me for one day, but I adore you and after my kingdom is restored, I could provide the life you deserve. I know I am not a prince..."

"Stop," Gwenyth commanded gently. "You are incredibly kind, and were it entirely up to me, I would gladly accept your offer. However, if we truly wish to be married, you must convince my mother to give her consent. My father would turn in his grave if I were to marry without Mother's permission."

"I am not rich, I am not a prince, and I am in the process of rebuilding my kingdom. She will never agree to such a match." The duke began to look defeated, but Gwenyth slid her arm through his and led him away, speaking in whispered tones.

"I stand amazed," Christopher said, eyes wide. "Whatever you did seems to be working."

"Now, if we can just get everything under control before..." Aurora trailed off as a high-pitched shrill voice echoed through the castle halls.

"Gwenyth! Where is my daughter? Gwenyth!"

"...her mother shows up," Aurora finished, glancing toward the princess in apprehension.

A herald stepped out the large palace doors and announced, "Her Majesty, Queen Tamera of Aliwyn, and His Royal Highness, Prince Edward of Tennia." To finish his announcement, the herald knocked the end of his scepter on the foyer just as a tall woman in a lavish purple gown, flowing robe and gleaming ornate crown swept past him. Her girth led Aurora to believe that she enjoyed her station immensely.

"Gwenyth!" she cried out as she seemed to float down the steps, arms outstretched in a phony gesture of caring.

Aurora shook her head as she watched Gwenyth collapse in horror, her knees turning to jelly at the sight of her mother. "Well, that didn't last long enough, did it?"

Christopher sighed. "Now it's in God's hands."

"Oh, don't start that again!" she protested.

He just shrugged as the queen enveloped Gwenyth in her arms. The duke stepped forward and bowed. "Your majesty, welcome to Romalia."

"Get away! Can you not see I have just been reunited with the daughter I thought I had lost? Why are you speaking?"

The duke bowed again and began to back away, his tail tucked firmly between his legs. Gwenyth shot him a helpless, pleading look, but he was at a loss for what to do.

"Thank goodness you are safe, my darling! I have been so worried about you!"

"I am alright, Mother, really. Our host has been most kind," she indicated the duke with a wave, but the queen merely dismissed him with a reproachful glance.

"I am sure he has," she muttered through clenched teeth. "Now that I know you are safe, we must return to Aliwyn and prepare for the wedding."

"The wedding?" Gwenyth asked, a quiver in her voice.

"Yes. I brought your fiancé with me. He was as anxious to see you as I was when we learned you were safe. Prince Edward!" she called back to the castle.

A young man, hardly old enough to hold a sword, appeared in the doorway by the herald. He had a small crown perched on top of his rather long blonde hair, and his milky white face was noticeably devoid of any hair or scars.

"He is but a child!" Gwenyth protested.

"Child or no, someday he will be a king … and you will be his queen," her mother announced with a devious smile.

"I do not care if he will be a king someday. He is still a child. Send him home to his mother. I shall not marry him." Both the prince and the duke breathed a visible sigh of relief at this announcement, but the queen looked utterly vexed.

"This is not up for discussion. The marriage has already been arranged. But let us not dwell on this news. Tell me, how did you manage to escape from that dreadful wizard?"

Gwenyth attempted to look cross. "I am not marrying the boy, end of discussion. And I did not escape, I was rescued." A little color returned to her cheeks.

The queen looked taken aback. "Rescued? How? Every knight or prince I sent failed."

"Here it comes," Aurora muttered, trying to flatten

Christopher's curly mess of hair with her hand, knowing full well they would soon be under scrutiny. He batted her hand away in annoyance.

Gwenyth smiled sweetly, and a twinkle of spunk appeared in her eye. "Allow me to present Sir Christopher of Calidore, the knight of legend, and Aurora of Beldain. ***They*** are responsible for my rescue."

The queen regarded them both skeptically, and Christopher bowed low in respect while Aurora stood tall and haughtily held her head high. "I see," she said slowly, "that the missing ingredient for your rescue was a disrespectful and defiant girl."

Aurora let a half smile cross her lips, giving her a feral, angry look. "Sorceress, actually, and I only show respect to those who deserve it."

"Aurora!" Christopher hissed under his breath.

The only thing that betrayed the queen's new unease at this announcement was that her eyes grew wider as she watched the heroes. "A knight … and a sorceress. And on behalf of what ruler and what kingdom did you rescue my daughter?"

"Uhh … none, Your Majesty. I have no allegiance to a specific kingdom. We rescued your daughter simply because she needed to be rescued."

The queen looked at Aurora. "And how do you fit?"

"I'm here to protect him from harm … and bad decisions, normally."

"Interesting." She turned back to her daughter, making sure not to turn her back on Aurora. "You truly refuse to marry Prince Edward?"

Gwenyth nodded meekly, smiling to herself at her tiny victory.

The queen glanced over at Christopher again. "It really is too bad that he is only a knight," she said with a sigh.

"I don't like where this is going," he muttered.

"However, he did rescue you. That means that he has won your hand in marriage and half the kingdom."

Christopher's jaw dropped in shock, his eyes nearly as wide as saucers. Aurora's face took on a disapproving look, while Duke William merely looked crushed. Released from his duty, the prince had already run away, hoping to avoid any further possible matrimonial entanglements.

Gwenyth took two frightened deep breaths before her eyes fell on the duke's face and an idea struck her. "Mother, I am a princess; surely I can make a better match than a knight who has no kingdom. Besides, Christopher is the famous knight of legend. He cannot settle down, he has a quest to fulfill. I could not possibly stand in the way of fate." Christopher breathed a sigh of relief and Aurora cocked her head to the side, wondering how the princess planned to turn everything around.

"But you must be married!" her mother protested. "The kingdom of Aliwyn needs an heir! I will not live forever ... unless," she trailed off, glancing at Aurora.

"Forget it!" the sorceress snapped, raising her right hand and pointing her finger in a warning gesture. "Don't make me do something you'll regret!"

The queen shuddered and turned back to her daughter. "Our kingdom will need a ruler after I am gone."

"I agree. The kingdom does need an heir. Fortunately, I have a solution. While he is not a prince, he is of higher nobility than a mere knight." She smiled slyly as she waved William forward. "May I present our host, Duke William III, of Romalia."

The queen turned an eye of reproach on the duke, whom she had dismissed until that moment. "Oh, really?" she smiled, sending a shiver down Christopher's spine. "The lord and master of all the land surrounding this castle..." She turned back to her daughter. "He seems to be doing quite well for himself," she said sarcastically.

Any hope that had been on either William or Gwenyth's faces had drained out of it. "But..." Gwenyth protested, "but a terrible ogre has been destroying the land. We were only able to defeat him two nights ago!"

"**We**?" the queen asked. "You do not mean to tell me that you were involved in such an undertaking? What did you do, throw your shoe at it and scream?"

Gwenyth looked defeated. "No, I contributed more than that."

Aurora stepped forward, a sly grin on her face. "She was instrumental in the creature's defeat. We couldn't have won without her." She then turned and looked directly into Gwenyth's eyes. *You can defeat her just as easily as we defeated the ogre. You already know how.*

Gwenyth's eyes went wide in surprise. She had heard Aurora's words inside her head even though the sorceress hadn't spoken a word. Suddenly, so many things made sense about the way Christopher and Aurora seemed to know what the other was thinking in battle. Aurora's words rang in her head, driving out all the doubt that her mother always seemed to fill her with.

"Besides, Your Majesty, within a year the land will be flourishing again," Aurora said, the conversation having continued while Gwenyth was lost in thought.

"I am supposed to believe the land will heal itself in less than a year?! That is impossible! It would take … magic … oh." Aurora continued to stare her down defiantly. "I should have guessed. But it does not matter! I forbid this marriage to take place!"

Gwenyth took a deep breath, the fire back in her eyes. "I do not care, Mother." Her voice was calm and quiet, but everyone heard her.

"What?!" the queen screeched, turning on her daughter.

Gwenyth didn't even flinch. "I said 'I do not care.' I refuse to let you marry me off to the richest prospect and make me miserable in the deal. I am going to marry William, and if you do not like it … I will have Aurora turn you into a toad until after the wedding night."

The queen's eyes went wide, betraying her fear of the sorceress' power. "You would not dare!"

"Would you prefer a ferret?" Aurora asked, reaching for her belt.

Christopher reached out and wrapped his hand around her upper arm, hoping to restrain her. "Don't," he hissed.

The queen took several fearful deep breaths and then composed herself. "Well, it appears I am severely outnumbered. Very well, if you wish to go from being a princess to a duchess, I shall not stop you."

Gwenyth smiled sweetly. "See, Mother, that is where you are wrong. As your only child, succession of Aliwyn falls to my son … no matter who his father is … if you want the kingdom to remain in the family. Since we both know that you enjoy being on the throne, you are not going to give that up any time soon to be married again, so I am not worried about a prince being born. Therefore, I will not allow you to declare this a morganatic marriage, which is what you are thinking. My son

will be your heir, even if you will not allow my husband to be elevated to a prince. Besides, my dowry and Aurora's magic will help get Romalia back to its former glory."

The duke's jaw dropped in surprise and the queen looked so mad that they thought she was going to explode. She looked back and forth between Gwenyth and the heroes. "I do not know what you have done to my daughter, but you will pay dearly for it!"

"I did nothing except remind her what her experiences had already taught her. You should be thankful that your daughter has spirit. Someday, it will be a virtue."

"I am finished with this conversation. Page! Escort me to my chambers. If I must endure a wedding, I intend to make myself comfortable."

As soon as the queen had disappeared into the castle, Gwenyth collapsed into William's arms laughing. "I cannot believe it! We won!"

Aurora smiled. "Congratulations, Princess. You're free."

Christopher bowed. "Your journey has found its end."

"Oh," she said, realizing for the first time that Christopher and Aurora would now be moving on. "Where will you go?"

"Northward," Aurora said, a small smile on her lips. "Did you want me to leave you some magic powder, just in case the queen gets out of hand?"

Gwenyth laughed. "No, I think the threat was enough to keep her in line. Thank you so much for everything. You have changed my life."

Aurora allowed the happy princess to hug her, and then Christopher bowed low over her hand and kissed it. "Farewell, Princess, and good luck. May God smile on you always."

Chapter XIV
A Wizard Encore

The travelers left the castle behind, Jonathan's saddle bags loaded down with supplies in return for the magic powder Aurora gave them to replenish the land. Aurora was riding Jonathan with Christopher walking and leading the horse at a leisurely pace.

After traveling for some time in awkward silence, Christopher glanced up at Aurora sheepishly. "I had gotten so used to having her talk that the silence is deafening."

She pursed her lips and shook her head in disbelief. "I never thought I'd say this, but I think you're right. It's almost ***too*** quiet."

"Come on, admit it."

"Don't say it! Don't even say it!" Aurora said curtly.

"You're going to miss her. Admit it."

"I will admit no such thing. I think I've aged tremendously since we met her."

"Funny," he said with a smile, "I think the same thing about you."

She glared at him in feigned indignation, but refrained from commenting. They continued on, the silence growing until all they could hear were the thunderous sounds of nature. Aurora could feel only the tiniest tug in the magic, barely pulling them in the direction they were meant to go, so they weren't hurrying, just journeying.

"Do you think she will be happy?" he asked, breaking the uncomfortable silence.

"Gwenyth? I think so. She's going to love being a duchess and someday a queen. She developed a new strength that has given her a different outlook on life. She wouldn't have been happy wandering around with us until we finally got around to taking her home. Besides, that's the life she's been raised to desire. She'll be fine."

Christopher nodded his head and glanced around at the clearing they had just entered. A small stream babbled across the north-east corner and the moon shone brightly overhead. "Camp here?"

Aurora glanced around and smiled. "Fire?"

"No problem."

They finished setting up camp in silence, with only Jonathan's nickering and the whispering of the brook to break the quiet. Finally, Christopher handed her a piece of bark with her dinner on it and he shook his head as he sat across the fire from her. "What I don't get is how we do all the work, we defeat the ogre, we get stuck escorting her around, she does nothing but complain and scream, and the duke falls for her. How does that make sense?"

"I know," she said with a smile, her voice full of mock envy, "some girls have all the luck. That doesn't explain why it bothers *you*, though."

He scrunched up his nose at her for pointing out the idiocy of his rantings. "It … it just does. But somehow I don't think you would be happy in her place."

"Really?" she grinned, her voice returning to normal. "What was your first clue?"

"Uh, well, I have trouble picturing you settling down, ruling a kingdom and raising children."

She shook her head. "No, you're right. I am not the family type. I enjoy being child-free and care-free."

He looked at her, his face taking on a more serious look. "So … where would you be happy?"

Aurora was taken aback, her eyes wide in surprise. "What do you mean? I'm happy here."

"You're telling me that you have no interest in meeting a nice prince and settling down in a castle if we ever break this curse? Assuming we ever do."

She laughed. "The curse will be broken someday; I wouldn't worry too much about that. However, a fairytale ending is not my style and you know it. Besides, I don't believe they can be achieved."

He looked at her in confusion. "I never understand half of what you say, you know that. What's a 'fairytale ending'?"

"You know how at the end of stories when the maiden gets her prince and they get married, the story ends 'happily ever after' just when their life together is beginning. That's because if they continued telling the story, it wouldn't end 'happily ever after.' Therefore, it's a fairytale ending."

"That's not true."

"Chris, think about it. Real life doesn't work that way. No real person can achieve 'happily ever after.' It's a realistic impossibility."

"You're making this up. How do you know that no real person can live 'happily ever after'? Have you asked every real person as they are leaving this earth to go to the next life if they lived 'happily ever after'? And if a person truly loves another, then they truly could live 'happily ever after,' through good times and bad, and perhaps even death couldn't part them."

"Don't get so emotional," she snapped, her green eyes flashing angrily. "You'd think I had told you God doesn't exist."

"Hey!"

"Believe me!" she said, raising her hand and pointing her finger at him in warning. "I know better than to start ***that*** argument with you!" The talisman crackled with energy. "I'm just saying that you might be overreacting. I don't believe fairytale endings happen in the real world. It's only for stories."

"Only for stories?! If that were true, then what hope for happiness is there to look forward to in life? If you don't believe in 'happily ever after,' does that mean you don't believe 'true love conquers all'?"

"You believe it pretty strongly, don't you? But if you knew what I know and had seen what I've seen, you wouldn't hold on to hope the way you do. It's pointless to believe in something that will never come to pass."

He shivered as a chill ran down his spine. "Did it get a little icy around here or is it just me?"

Her green eyes were almost glacial blue as she seemed to stare right through him. "Icy? You haven't seen anything yet!"

As the words left her mouth, she stood up to walk away and suddenly the noisy crackle of the fire was silenced as the flames turned to ice. Christopher glanced from side to side and noticed that a frost had settled over the entire clearing. "Aurora, cut it out. Remember, Lysette said Varuk can track the talisman if you use it."

She just gave him a defeated glare. He glanced up at the

sky and a chill wind whipped through his curls as a cloud cover swiftly moved in from nowhere to block out the moon.

"I'm not doing that," she said, answering his unspoken question.

Without warning, lightning struck their frozen fire, sending it blazing back to life and instantly thawing the clearing out. "Wow, that was strange." When she didn't answer, he turned to face her and discovered she had been turned to stone, her face frozen in an expression of confusion and her lips pursed as if to frame a question. "Uh oh, not good."

A wild cackling sound began behind him and Christopher immediately knew what had happened. "So, you went crawling back to your master after all?" he asked as he turned to face Varuk.

The aged wizard smiled, his black teeth spread apart in glee. "My master was very disappointed that I lost my talisman, but he was delighted to discover who had taken it from me."

"If you're here to get it back, I think you're going about it all wrong. See, it's hard to get the talisman back when you have turned it and her to stone."

Varuk's eyes narrowed. "Do you honestly believe that I came here for the talisman? You stole my trophy. She was to have been my bride. Her youth was to have helped me be reborn. But you and your magical guide had to step in. You stole my trophy!"

Christopher sighed. "You said that already."

Varuk growled. "Do not speak, Mortal! You will make me lose my train of thought!" The wizard tugged at his grizzled beard, causing his robes to move just enough that Christopher noticed a red talisman hanging around his neck.

The talisman. It's the source of his power.

Christopher heard her voice loud and clear in his head even though there was no way she could have spoken. He glanced over at his partner and discovered that the entire statue was glowing a faint green. *At least you aren't completely helpless.*

That would be the day.

"Since you found it necessary to relieve me of my trophy," Varuk was saying, "my master has asked me to relieve you of your trophy and bring her before him."

"Yeah, I'm not sure you should be calling her a trophy. She might take offense to that."

The wizard glared at him and then turned his head slightly to glare at the statue. "That's all she ever was before ... and she shall be so again. My master bids me to reclaim his property ... and I have."

Out of the corner of his eye, Christopher noticed the intensity of the statue's glow was increasing. "She's going to make you very sorry you said that."

The wizard grinned evilly. "She can't do anything to me. And my master will put her back in her place. But you, you aren't part of the solution. I'm to take care of you before I deliver my master's prize."

Christopher glanced down to draw his sword and noticed the blade was glowing green, just like the talisman. He found himself smiling in spite of their situation.

Varuk stared at Sir Christopher in astonishment. "You foolish mortal! Do you truly believe you can survive my wrath without your sorceress to help you?!"

He pulled his sword into a defensive position as Varuk hurled a spell at him like a lightning bolt. To the surprise of both of them, the spell seemed to wrap itself around the sword and dissipate, causing the glow to ripple and crackle and become a brighter green. Christopher's face betrayed both his surprise and delight as he prepared to fend off another blow.

Varuk looked shocked. "That's impossible!" he yelled in anger, hurling another spell at Christopher with the same results as the first. "You're a mortal!" He hurled another spell. "You don't have that kind of power!" He hurled another spell. "How are you doing this?!" Another spell. "She can't help you!" he shrieked, sounding as if he was really trying to convince himself. "She can't perform magic like … ***that***!" He was so frustrated that he gestured at the statue with both hands, turning his attention away from Christopher just long enough that he could swing his sword and break the red talisman.

"No, you fool, do you know what you've done?!"

Christopher watched him curiously, because before his very eyes, Varuk seemed to be shrinking.

"You didn't win!" he was screaming, now the size of a child. "This isn't over! He'll make you pay!" Christopher bent down to look the wizard in the face, but by that time he had been reduced to the size of a cat so Christopher picked him up by the back of his robes. "He hates to lose, especially to mortals!" He had now shrunk to the size of a mouse and his voice was squeaking to match. "You'll never be free of him, so long as you associate with her!" Then, with a puff of smoke, he shrank into nothing and was gone.

"That was strange," he said, replacing his sword in its sheath.

That's the least of our problems.

He spun around in surprise and discovered that she was ***still*** a statue.

He cast an independent spell.

Christopher shook his head and walked over to the statue. "So, what do we do? Can you reverse it?"

Is my clothing stone as well as my skin?

He nodded his head.

Then you can't use the powders and I can't do anything. Any ideas?

He nodded his head slightly, lost in thought. Once he had wandered around to the other side of the fire, he knelt down and bowed his head in prayer. "Unless you have a better idea, not one word." He knew Aurora would be rolling her eyes at him if she could.

He stayed like that for quite some time, and by the time he had finished the fire had died down to coals. He opened his eyes and stared at the glowing coals, when suddenly, the flames jumped back to life. As he watched, an image began to form in the fire of two people leaning in for a kiss.

His eyes went wide and his mouth fell open slightly. "Truly you jest!" As the words left his mouth, the fire flared up again. "Alright. I get the hint."

He drew in a deep breath and then released it as he stood up and walked over to the statue. He glanced up at the sky. "I hope this works," he muttered, and as the words left his mouth, the fire flared up for the third time. He sighed in defeat. "I apologize in advance for my forward behavior," he whispered as he leaned forward and kissed the cold stone lips.

To his surprise, almost immediately the lips became warm

and soft. He quickly drew back in embarrassment and his cheeks turned red.

Aurora let out a sigh. “About time! Left me waiting forever for you and your divine solutions!”

He sat down in a huff and covered his eyes with his left hand out of frustration. He then ran his hand back through his hair and brought it up to rest under his chin. “You never change.”

She simply smiled. “The good news is he’s gone for good this time,” she said, changing the subject.

“I suppose it’s too much to hope that you will explain all of his cryptic statements.”

“Hope all you want. Doesn’t mean I’ll talk.”

He sighed. “Well, good night then.”

“Goodnight, Chris.” Turning her eyes to the forest to keep watch, she added quietly, “and thank you.”

He couldn’t help but smile as he drifted off to sleep.

Chapter XV
Evil Lurks on the Horizon

The next morning they started off on another journey. As always, they didn't really know where they were going, they just let the magic guide them.

They traveled for two days without incident or without running into anyone who needed help, and it was starting to bother Christopher. "I don't understand it. We have rarely hit a lull since we were cursed."

"Maybe evil is on vacation," she joked, flying level with his head.

He raised his eyebrows at her. "I highly doubt evil is organized enough to all go on vacation at once."

"Well, if they can organize crime, why can't they organize evil?" When he simply stared at her with a blank look on his face, she sighed, "Nevermind. Look, we've been at this for years. Just enjoy the down time."

"Down time?" Christopher muttered as she flew out of sight. "Do you ever understand what she's talking about?" Jonathan just snorted his negation.

The pull of the magic was stronger by then, but the direction wasn't entirely clear, so Aurora had to fly in large sweeping arcs overhead frequently in order to keep them on course. During one of the small spans of time she spent flying nearby, Christopher caught her off-guard with a question.

"Do you ever wonder where we would be, what life would be like, if we had never been cursed?"

Without glancing over at him, she answered simply, "We'd be dead."

He scrunched his nose and pursed his lips in annoyance. "No, I mean, what if Lionel's kingdom hadn't been overrun by evil? Where would we be?"

Her eyes took on a faraway look. "What does it matter? Lionel's kingdom fell, we were the only survivors and we ***were*** cursed. What good does it do to dwell on the past and wonder 'what if?' You don't see me daydreaming and envisioning a different life."

"It was just a simple question. You have no imagination," he frowned. "But you raise an interesting point. Why were ***we*** the only survivors?"

"What?" Her eyes grew wide in panic.

"Why did you save me and not King Lionel?"

"Because it was not your fate to die that day and because you were my friend."

"Then why not save both of us?"

"The magic I used to save us was so difficult to maintain that to expand it to contain a third person would have drained me to the point of death … and if I had died, the spell would have collapsed."

"I still don't understand why you saved me and not someone else."

"I wish I had now!" She transformed into her human form and stood blocking the center of the path, her hair a brilliant shade of burgundy. "Would you prefer I ***had*** saved someone else?!"

"That's not what I meant and you know it! I just want to know why you chose me!"

"Would it make you happy to hear me say that I saved you because you were the only person who wasn't convinced I was contracted with the devil in some way, and that includes King Lionel?! Do you want to hear that I'm not sorry they're all dead?! That I hope they rot in hell?! Fine, I said it, now let it go!" And with a puff of smoke, she was gone.

"Aurora!" he called out to the empty forest. He dismounted and slumped to the ground against a tree, dejected. "Why does she have to be so stubborn and take everything so personally?"

Alone with Jonathan and the sounds of the forest, he decided to make camp. He was unsure of when she'd come back, but he knew it was her habit to reappear where she thought he'd be. On occasion it took her more than one try, but she was normally pretty good at anticipating his whereabouts. He stared at the flickering flames of the fire and contemplated everything she had said, still unsure about so many things. He looked up at Jonathan. "There's so much I still don't know or understand about her." Suddenly, Jonathan began shifting from one leg to another in panic.

"That makes her no different from every other woman," a small voice growled. Christopher raised his brows and searched the surrounding forest before he stared at Jonathan with a brow raised quizzically.

"I beg your pardon?" he said, his left hand slowly reaching for his sword. He was waiting expectantly for the voice to speak again when he noticed a rustling in the bushes by Jonathan's forelegs and a small grey wolf cub tumbled out and rolled to a stop, his tongue lolled out in enthusiasm.

"You said you don't understand her and I said that makes her like all other women. She may be a sorceress but she's still just a woman."

Christopher scoffed, slowly sliding his hand away from his sword. "It's not the woman part I don't understand. And how do you know she's a sorceress? How long have you been listening?"

"Well..." the little wolf said, crouching down and putting his head on his front paws with a guilty look on his face, "it wasn't intentional. You see, I'm lost and I was trying to get my bearings but I hurt my paw and you guys were kinda loud and I thought you could help me and then she disappeared..."

"Whoa, slow down. How can I help you?"

"Well, I can't get my bearings and I can't really walk and I was howling all night and my family still hasn't found me and I thought if I could help you then you would help me..."

"Wait ... okay, how is it you think you can help me?"

"Well, my master is very powerful, and I figured if you didn't want to be saddled with ***her*** forever, maybe you should talk to someone about breaking the curse."

"How do you know we are cursed?" he asked, suddenly suspicious.

The cub looked sheepish. "Are there any knights who travel with a sorceress for a companion other than the fated Sir Christopher of Calidore?"

Christopher opened his mouth to retort and realized the truth behind the cub's words. "No, I suppose not. But why should I talk to your master about breaking the curse? It will lift itself eventually."

"Suit yourself," the cub answered around a mouthful of fur

as he tried to alleviate an itch in his side. "I just thought you'd want another option in case it doesn't lift itself. But, if you want to be optimistic, fine." He stopped biting his side and looked at the knight earnestly. "But, if you don't want my master's help, will you still help me get home?"

Christopher's face softened. "Of course. Where is home, or rather, ***what*** is home? I'm not trying to find a cave in this forest, am I?"

"Oh no. I live in a castle … I just can't find it."

"Well … the magic ***was*** leading us in this direction. Let's take a chance."

Jonathan let out a worried whinny and pulled Christopher's bag of armor from the saddle bag with his teeth, dropping it on the ground with a loud clang.

Christopher looked at the horse in confusion. "I don't need it. We're just taking the cub home."

Jonathan let out a frantic whinny and stamped his front hooves on the ground.

"The master won't care if you wear your armor."

Christopher glanced from cub to horse and back. "Knights normally only wear armor in battle. I don't want anyone to think I'm attacking."

"Don't worry. I'll make your intentions known once we're close enough."

Christopher sighed in defeat and began to don his armor. "Paranoid stallion. Sometimes I get the feeling you just enjoy watching me be uncomfortable." Jonathan snorted in anger and pawed the ground in agitation.

After Christopher was armed completely, the wolf cub wandered into the bushes while Christopher broke camp.

"What do you think?" he asked the horse in whispered tones. Jonathan snorted and jerked his head away angrily. "Look, I'm just helping someone in need. And if I manage to get a few questions answered in the meantime, then I have come out ahead." Jonathan snorted again. "Don't worry so much," he chastised, placing his armor-clad hand on the horse's shoulder in reassurance.

The cub tumbled out of the bushes. "All set?"

Christopher nodded and the great horse knelt down, even though they could tell it was under protest. Christopher scooped up the cub in his arms and climbed into the saddle, the three travelers taking off at a brisk canter.

After some time, they reached a meadow with a large black castle in it, surrounded by a moat. As soon as they cleared the trees, the cub began howling with delight and a chorus of howls answered him from inside the castle walls. The cub began squirming. "My master wishes to welcome you and thank you." The drawbridge began lowering. "Your horse can wait here if you wish. I'm told the meadow has some of the finest grass for grazing found anywhere."

The drawbridge touched down with a thud and Christopher shrugged. "If you're sure he will be safe I guess he can stay out here."

Christopher dismounted and patted his steed on the shoulder reassuringly. "Don't worry. He probably wants to say thank you and tell me that he has no answers for me and then he will send me on my way."

Jonathan nickered worriedly, but could do nothing to dissuade the hero as he began to cross the drawbridge on the wolf cub's heels.

About halfway across the drawbridge, Christopher turned to smile at Jonathan. "See you soon," he called.

The horse was so worried that he wasn't even interested in savoring the lush green grasses of the meadow. He could only watch and wait.

Christopher stepped into the entryway of the castle and stopped dead in his tracks. "I'm beginning to get a bad feeling about this," he muttered as a feeling of dread spread from the pit of his stomach to all his limbs and pinpricks of danger went shooting up his spine.

"As well you should," a deep, sickly-sweet male voice said from the shadows as the portcullis slammed shut and flames shot up from the moat to form a barrier, the drawbridge crumbling to ash in the heat of the flames. "You won't be needing that," the voice said, and with a painful flash of light, Christopher found himself stripped of his armor and his wrists manacled to the floor, with only his sword lying nearby.

He tugged at the chains to test their strength.

"Oh, really now. It's useless to struggle," the voice spoke again. "If I wanted you dead, it would have happened already. You aren't the one I'm after. You're simply bait for a much bigger prize."

Christopher tugged at the chains again. "What do you want with Aurora?!" he demanded of the darkness.

"Ohh, very good. Ten points for our heroic captive. Aurora and I had a bargain … and she broke it. I want retribution." The embodiment of the voice stepped out of the shadows. He was tall and thin, taller than Christopher, and with his long black hair pulled back into a sleek ponytail and his glowing red eyes blazing from deep within his face, he was the epitome of evil. He was dressed all in black with a cape thrown across his shoulders in a very regal style.

"I'm in trouble!" Christopher muttered hastily.

The dark lord grinned evilly. "You most certainly are. Now, don't forget to call for help." And with a wave of his hand, Christopher found himself in the center of a large gladiator arena.

With a loud roar, two lions immediately leapt at him. He barely had time to roll for his sword before they were upon him. "Aurora!"

The dark lord smiled from his vantage point. "What a good mortal."

The moment the flames had sprung up from the moat, Jonathan had taken off at a full gallop to get back to where he knew Aurora would be when Christopher called for help. He arrived by the remnants of the fire only moments after she appeared. She glanced around in confusion and then glared at the horse. "What's happened? Where is he? Speak, I command you!" she said with a wave of her hand.

"He's too honest for his own good!" the horse sputtered. "A little lost wolf cub offered information about the curse in return for help in returning to his master. He didn't think it would hurt to ask and the cub needed help so he went and now he's trapped in a black castle with a moat of mystical flames at the end of the path."

She let out a long, deep sigh. "If he's still alive, I'm gonna kill him!"

"Can I go back to being just a dumb animal now?"

She waved her hand again, this time as if collecting smoke

into her balled fist. “Meet me there.” With a bright flash of light, she was gone and the horse took off running once again.

Aurora arrived in the entry hall of the dark lord’s castle with a dramatic puff of smoke. A deep, booming laughter filled the hall, echoing from every corner. She sighed. “Dispense with the cheap theatrics! You have my traveling companion! I am here to retrieve him!” she bellowed at the laughing darkness.

“Aurora of Beldain, if you want the knight’s freedom as well as his life, then you must earn it.” A glowing orb appeared floating before her eyes, and within it she could see Christopher, without his armor, battling for his life.

“Hold on, Chris,” she whispered.

“Oh, please!” the dark lord said patronizingly, stepping from the shadows. “Don’t tell me you actually have feelings for the mortal!”

Aurora straightened herself up to her full height. “More than I ever had for you, Léon.” She nearly spat his name in contempt.

“Oh, come now. None of that. You know you missed me.”

“No, I missed your power … but I no longer need it.”

He smirked. “You might think you don’t need it, but you still crave it. I can see it in your eyes.”

“Actually, what you’re seeing is me attempting to keep my dinner down at the sight of you.”

He laughed at her. “You truly have become weak and pathetic.”

“No more than you: resorting to meddling and trickery to get me here.”

His red eyes blazed greedily. “How I’ve missed you. I knew

if I could just get you back here, all the old feelings would come rushing back."

She let out a curt laugh. "***Your*** feelings may have come rushing back. All ***I*** feel is revulsion."

His facial expression glazed over like a piece of ice, his glee suddenly gone. "Perhaps you'll feel differently after you complete the tasks I've chosen for you. So, let's bring an element of fun to the proceedings. Before your dear Sir Christopher tires and gets eaten, your first task is to bring me a piece of the sky."

Aurora's eyebrows went up. "A piece of the sky; is that all? Nice to see you're still reaching for the stars." She vanished in a puff of smoke, transporting herself halfway around the world. She found herself in the swirling sands of the Gobi desert, using her magic to search for a rock that she knew had fallen from space and hit the earth the night before. The swirling sands subsided and Aurora spotted the chasm it had gouged in the earth as it landed. Using her magic to create a whirlwind, Aurora lifted the glowing rock from its resting place. With a puff of smoke, she transported herself, the rock and the swirling winds back to the castle.

Léon stood his ground, cape dancing wildly as the whirlwind slowly subsided, dropping the glowing rock at his feet. Several wisps of burgundy hair blew across her face until the wind died, her angry green eyes unflinching. "I've brought you a piece of the sky," she hissed. "This is as close as you'll come to grasping the stars."

He laughed. "Sounds like someone isn't in the mood to play my game. Maybe we should up the stakes." With a snap of his fingers, four more lions appeared in the arena with

Christopher. He already had several wounds and was swinging his sword with less vigor.

"If he dies, you will suffer for all eternity," she growled, her burgundy hair streaked with black.

"Then I suggest you stop stalling. Your next task: bring me a child's laugh."

"Your intelligence really is in question now. A child's laugh?"

"I'm not picky. Any form you choose."

She scowled at him and vanished from his court.

"She hasn't changed," he smiled. "All the better."

"But she has the stink of humanity on her," a large direwolf, nearly the size of a lion, growled from the shadows. "She may have changed more than you realize."

"She will be mine … willingly. An eon of contemplation will see to that. And once the knight is dead…"

"We shall see," the wolf growled, unaware that her cub had been listening nearby.

Aurora returned soon after, holding a jar in her hand. "Not that laughter could survive long here, but…" she hissed, tossing the jar at his head. Léon deftly reached up and plucked it from the air. Inside the jar, a tiny fairy beat against the glass, pleading to be let out.

"Ah, a baby's first laugh begets a fairy. Very resourceful. You *do* know that you have sealed her doom?"

"A price I pay for Chris' life."

"Very well. Your final task: make this potion."

A piece of parchment began floating in the air right in front of her face. She scanned the ingredients list and was horrified at the rarity of most of the items, but she didn't let it show. She directed a level stare at him. "If I get all these ingredients and make the potion, Chris is free?"

He appeared to consider it. "Very well. If you do as I ask ... and I know the potion works, then I shall release the knight."

The left corner of her mouth twitched and went up slightly. "I'll be right back." She vanished in a puff of smoke.

"Do you really intend to release the knight?"

Léon grinned evilly. "Of course. Right before her eyes I will release him from his earthly bonds and send him to the afterlife."

The wolf cub, still concealed, managed to stifle a gasp.

"I volunteer to be the agent of his demise," the large wolf growled, getting to her feet.

"Perfect."

Aurora appeared in the clearing, across from the burning moat. "How am I going to do this?" she muttered, examining the parchment more closely. She needed a dragon scale, phoenix tear, griffin feather, unicorn oil, ground hen's teeth, rainbow powder from a leprechaun, fairy dust, liquid fire, and the boiling blood of a chimera. There were detailed instructions on what to mix when and how much. She found herself trying to slow her breathing as panic set in. Most of the items were rare but with some hard work she would be able to acquire them. However, in all her travels she had never encountered a leprechaun and she had no idea where to get their rainbow powder. Also, the liquid fire was something she had only heard stories about and had no idea how to track down a source. She started with the less impossible tasks: collecting a tear from the pet phoenix of a wizard she used to know, collecting a discarded scale from the lair of a sleeping dragon, visiting a shady apothecary in the orient for a vial of unicorn oil and the ground hen's teeth, outsmarting a griffin to pluck one of its golden feathers before it killed her, and imploring the princess of the fairies to aid her with fairy dust even though she had just captured one of her subjects. The boiling chimera blood was a little trickier, and she managed to get her left arm slashed to the bone by its razor sharp claws as she extracted blood while avoiding its three fire breathing mouths.

She stopped to bandage herself and decide what to do about the two missing ingredients. She found her thoughts drifting to her mentor. "What would Lysette do if presented with this problem?" she mused as she applied salve to her wound and hissed in pain. Then she laughed bitterly. "Who am I kidding? Lysette would have seen the future, known what she would need, and … acquired it … long before … the situation arrived." Absently, Aurora reached for the two pouches of unidentified powder that Lysette had included in their satchel. The first was iridescent and glittered every color of the rainbow when the light hit it. "I wonder…" She sprinkled a tiny bit in the grass and immediately a tiny rainbow sprang from that spot and reached high into the heavens. Aurora shook her head in disbelief and examined the second powder. It was like fine crushed black glass and felt warm to the touch. She added a pinch to the dew that had collected on a nearby leaf and the liquid on the leaf immediately burst into flame. She scoffed. "I don't believe this. Liquid fire … just add water. She knew! That sneaky…" She breathed in several frustrated breaths. "Forget it. Worry about it later. To work."

She found the instructions tedious and complicated, but she finally finished the dark lord's potion and poured it into a small vial. "If only I knew the potion's purpose, I'd feel a lot better about what's about to happen," she muttered as she transported herself back to the castle.

"Where is Chris?!" she demanded, holding the vial up so he could see it.

"Give me the vial and I'll let him go," he said eagerly, stretching out his hand.

Her fist clenched tightly around the bottle and her hair began to be evenly streaked with black. "I'm not letting go of it until I see Chris!"

The dark lord snapped his fingers and Christopher appeared, sword in hand, his wrists manacled once again. He collapsed to the floor in exhaustion, revealing the bloody claw marks all across his back. His left hand could barely hold his sword because of all the bites on his wrist. He looked up at Aurora and she saw the fire return to his eyes at the sight of her.

"Now give me the vial!" the dark lord demanded at the top of his voice.

Aurora leveled a stare at him and made a move to hand it over when the wolf cub burst out of the shadows. "Don't do it!"

Christopher glanced from the dark lord back to Aurora. "He's going to imprison you!" he cried out, suddenly catching on to what was happening.

"Kill him!" the dark lord commanded.

The she-wolf leapt out of the shadows and cuffed her cub, sending him flying across the room to crumple in a heap against the far wall. "Gladly," she growled as she prepared to pounce on the fallen knight.

All of Aurora's hair turned jet black as she flung a spell at Christopher that unlocked his bonds. "I asked you to let him go," she said with a powerful calm to her voice. "You're going to regret that you didn't."

Christopher barely had time to bring his sword up as the wolf leapt at him, running her through with the momentum of her leap, and causing her to land on top of him, instantly dead. Her back legs twitched once, clawing his legs as he attempted to push her huge corpse off him.

Léon gaped at Aurora in surprise. He saw lightning crackling across the surface of her green eyes and some of her loose wisps of hair beginning to stand on end. Her hands were held slightly away from her sides, her left hand tightly clenched around the vial. Then he smiled. "I knew the darkness was still in you. Embrace it! Come back to me!"

"You messed with the wrong human if you were trying to win me back!"

The dark lord drew in a sharp breath as his eyes fell on the steadily growing green glow that she seemed to be generating. "The talisman!" he gasped, fear showing through his confidence for the first time.

The talisman around her neck was glowing bright green and the strength of the magic it was generating pulsated throughout the room. Aurora's eyes took on an intense light, as if her eyes had been removed from her head and this light was now trying to escape through the holes, and she was chanting in Gaelic. The dark lord was grasped by her magic and lifted off the floor. He began spinning end over end above Christopher's head as the knight finally managed to get out from under the dead direwolf and crawl across the floor to check on the cub. He struggled to his feet, cradling the wounded pup in his arms and watched the unfolding scene with misgiving.

"You've made my life miserable for the last time!" Aurora hollered, the wind and electricity bringing her voice to a screeching level.

"Use his own potion against him!" Christopher cried out, straining to be heard over the scream of the storm Aurora's anger had conjured.

To stop Christopher from giving the sorceress any more helpful tips, the dark lord cast a spell that caused him to become frozen. Aurora turned to see Christopher, cub cradled in his right arm, frozen in the act of trying to draw his sword from the carcass of the she-wolf. She became so enraged that she invoked the strength and powers of all the sorceresses of the order of Beldain, past and present. With the talisman to intensify it, the power was teetering on the brink of being beyond her control.

The dark lord was screaming curses at her now, trying everything he could think of to distract her from what she was about to do. "You can't do it! This is too dark, especially for you! You can't take my life!"

She took a deep breath and stared at him, her eyes white with electricity and her hair as black as the night sky. When she finally spoke, it was barely above a whisper but the power behind it projected it loud enough to be heard over the storm, "Then I'll soon see you in hell."

As the words left her mouth, she threw the vial at the

ground below him. She then threw her head back and began chanting, spreading her hands wide and allowing the storm to lift her off the ground. As the spilt liquid began to evaporate, the green smoke wrapped itself around the dark lord and imprisoned him in a glowing green orb.

As soon as the dark lord's magic was bound, Christopher was released from the spell. He looked up and immediately hit the ground, curling his body around the cub to protect him and covering his own head with his arms.

Lightning began to arc from Aurora's outstretched hands to the orb, causing the surface to begin to boil. Léon, who had been banging on the wall silently begging her to release him, was now trying desperately to get away from the walls as the magic began to close in on him.

"Aurora! Stop!" Christopher screamed into the storm. "Don't do it!"

The lightning stopped and Christopher lifted his head, hoping that she had decided to stop the assault and show mercy. Her hair was all wildly standing on end and the lightning continued to flash across the orbs of light where her eyes should have been. Christopher slowly got to his feet and then glanced at the orb. Lightning was streaking all across its surface as if it was about to explode any moment.

"Farewell, Lover," Aurora said with no emotion in her voice as the surface of the orb cracked into a thousand pieces. Christopher shielded his eyes as the orb exploded, dispelling a cloud of magic in all directions.

When the orb shattered, Aurora's magic dissipated and she collapsed in exhaustion. Christopher barely had time to cross the distance and catch her as she fell from the air.

"Let's get out of here," she whispered, weakly wrapping her arms around his neck just before she fainted.

The wounded knight scooped her up in his arms and he fumbled with his injured hand for the pouch on her belt that had the special powder in it. As he sprinkled the powder on her and she began to shrink, he brushed her hair off her face. "I am so sorry," he whispered back.

Once she had completely transformed, he draped her gently across his shoulders, stopped to retrieve his bloody sword and the wounded cub, and then walked out of the castle, leaving his armor, her past and the stench of evil behind them.

Chapter XVI
The Past Relived

Christopher staggered out of the castle, bloody, battered and completely exhausted. Jonathan was waiting nervously in the clearing. At the sight of his master, the horse let out a relieved whinny and dashed across the grass to kneel in front of the knight, as eager to leave the area as the rest of them were. Christopher pulled himself into the saddle, unable to bring himself to make camp with his injuries, especially so close to the lingering presence of evil.

He had placed Aurora in a saddle bag and the pup across his lap so that he could try to stop the bleeding on his left arm. As Jonathan trotted through the forest, they could vaguely hear the hoof beats of another horse nearby.

"Sounds like we're not the only ones on the move tonight," he commented. Aurora was too tired to answer.

"I'm sorry," the wolf cub whimpered. "I didn't know it was a trap."

Christopher scratched the pup behind his ears with his injured left hand while still keeping pressure on his arm with his right. "Hey, at least you put in a valiant effort to help save us. Thank you for that."

The pup looked up at him with sorrow in his eyes. "As soon as I'm well … I'll be on my way."

Christopher smiled weakly. "You're welcome to travel with us as long as you like."

The cub nodded slowly and put his head down on his front paws. "I'd like that. But, if I am to travel with you, perhaps you should come up with a name for me."

"You don't have a name?"

"No, I do. I just decided to leave it behind with my old life."

"Let me think on that," he said as the other hoof beats came closer.

They entered a clearing and came upon the other rider. He was dressed in a regal tunic with a cloak flowing out behind him. His horse was all black and held itself in a way that announced it was from royal stables. The rider bowed slightly. "Kind sir, I seek Sir Christopher of Calidore and am told he and his companion had been seen in the area. Have you encountered him on your travels?"

Christopher sighed. "Frequently, I'm afraid. I am he."

"Fortune has indeed smiled upon me today," he said, drawing nearer. "I am Prince Guillaume of the kingdom of Maystaire. My father requests an audience with you and your mysterious companion of legend. He wishes to hear tell of your heroic deeds."

"We are weary and wounded…"

"Say no more. Please, come with me to my father's castle. There you will find soft beds, plenty of food, and the royal surgeon will dress your wounds. Where is your companion?"

"She's here," he smiled, patting the saddle bag.

"She's riding cargo while 'man's best friend' rides coach," Aurora grumbled from the saddle bag.

Christopher and the pup looked at each other in confusion before following the prince through the forest. After the better part of an hour had passed, and several more riders had joined their entourage, they came upon a grand castle atop a hill with a village spanning out around it.

Aurora let out a small sigh of relief at the sight of it. As Jonathan trotted across the drawbridge, a feeling of comfort overwhelmed the travelers. At the prince's direction, Jonathan was taken off to the royal stables to be pampered, and the others were ushered inside. Aurora the ferret was given her own room and placed on the bed to recover while Christopher and the pup were escorted to another room and the surgeon called. Christopher's wounds were extensive, and the surgeon was horrified by the angry scars all over his torso, but finally he was left alone with the cub to rest.

"She'll be okay … right?" the pup asked, jumping up onto the bed to lie down next to Christopher after some difficulty.

The knight sighed. "I hope so. I'd hate to think that my mistake brought her to serious harm." He checked the dressing on his arm and discovered that he was starting to bleed through, but he was so tired that he didn't care. "I never realized how much I take her magic for granted," he muttered as he crawled into bed. "I can't even think of the last time I had to dress a battle wound." The pup laid his head on his paws beside the hero and soon they were both asleep.

Christopher awoke in the middle of the night to the sounds of the pup trying to claw his way back onto the bed.

"She's dead! She's dead! I think she's dead!" the pup clamored, still unable to climb in his haste with his injured paw.

Christopher threw back the covers and pulled on a tunic as he ran barefoot down the hall to the room they had provided the sorceress. As he went, he flexed his injured arm and noticed someone had redressed his wounds while he slept.

He arrived at her door and didn't even bother to knock, pushing the heavy door open the rest of the way. It took his eyes a moment to adjust to the dim light. There were tall candles lit all over the room, and her lightning burned clothes were lying in a heap at the foot of the bed. A black ermine dressing gown was draped over a nearby chair and the fire in the fireplace had burned down to coals. Then he saw her. She had changed back into human form, her red hair wild and still streaked with black highlights. She was wearing a simple white shift and there were bandages placed sporadically on her limbs, neck and face. She was curled up like a newborn foal in the center of the bed, her face an ashen shade of grey. He rushed to her bedside, taking her hand in his and brushing his other hand across her cheek.

"You're not dead," he said, his voice barely above a whisper. Her breathing was shallow, her skin was clammy to the touch, and she was shaking slightly. He pulled a blanket up over her. "God," he prayed, "please let her be okay. Please tell me I haven't killed her." He closed his eyes and pressed her hand to his forehead.

A small sound escaped her lips before her body was wracked with coughs. His eyes flew open and he found himself staring into her open eyes, which were the same grey color as her skin. He leaned closer, hoping to catch what she was trying to say.

"Aurora? What is it?"

"Don't worry, Hero," she said, her voice barely audible. "You can't get rid of me that easily. But … I'm burned, not cold," she whimpered, trying to shrug off the blanket.

"Oh! Sorry!" he said as he gently lifted it off her.

The cub limped into the room. "Is she...?" he asked, afraid to finish the question.

Christopher smiled. "She's going to make it." The cub crawled into his lap and curled up.

The next morning, the servants found the three travelers sleeping soundly, Aurora still curled up on the bed, Christopher sitting on the ground beside it with his head cradled on his injured arm and the pup curled up on his lap. They woke them and quickly ushered Christopher back to his room.

"Wait!" Aurora called. "The purple powder!" She coughed. "Add some of it to the salve for his wounds. And bring me some wine."

The servants did as she asked and helped the travelers to freshen up. Christopher and the pup both had their wounds dressed with the new salve and the results were almost immediate. Christopher flexed his arm and was delighted to discover that in spite of all the damage, he could still use it if he had to fight. The pup could put weight on his paw for the first time in days.

Christopher quickly dressed himself in the clothes provided by their hosts, strapping on his sword belt, and rushed down the hall to wait for Aurora.

The servants brought her the requested wine and she added some of the purple powder. She then drained the goblet in one gulp. The servants had then helped her to bathe and dress with eyes wide and mouths agape because the burns that had covered most of her body were gone.

Christopher was pacing nervously in the hall when the servants finally emerged. "She's asking for you, Sir," one of the girls curtseyed.

He drew in a deep breath, pushed open the heavy door and stepped into her bedchamber. She was wearing a simple blue gown trimmed in fur their hosts had provided and she was sitting quietly in a chair near the fire. She looked up when he entered, and although he could tell she was still weak, the fire and passion had returned to her brilliant green eyes. "It's nice to see you're feeling better," he said with a small smile, sitting down across from her.

She nodded. "How's your arm?" she asked, her voice still quiet and now filled with concern.

"I will live. What about you?"

"Lysette's new powder," she said with a smile, and he was happy to see the burns had healed.

He folded his hands in his lap and stared at them for a moment before he met her pained gaze. "We need to talk."

"They're expecting us at breakfast," she said hastily, trying to stand.

"Sit down!" he commanded, getting to his feet. The power in his voice caught her off guard and she stared up at him with a guilty look on her face. "What was all that about?! ***Now*** I need to know."

She sighed in defeat. "I'm sorry! I was afraid you wouldn't trust me."

"The past is the past. I understand that better than most people. But when it tries to kill me, I have a right to know why."

"He hated you. He thought you had stolen me away from him."

"Excuse me? Who?"

"Léon … the dark lord. I was going to be his bride."

Christopher felt his jaw drop open in shock. "You were going to marry … ***him***? He's evil!"

Aurora sighed again. "I know! You think I don't know that?!"

"Magic doesn't choose sides," he said quietly, almost to himself. "Aide is never one-sided."

"I beg your pardon?"

His eyes focused on Aurora's face. "I'm your penance." She sucked her breath in but he didn't stop there. "Lysette reminded you that you're not supposed to take sides, so you started helping King Lionel and then me to make up for helping Léon. That's why you never complain about the curse. You see me as your penance."

She put her face in her hands. "That's not it at all. Léon and I … we terrorized humans … we played chess with them as the pawns for fifty years. I thought Lysette was wrong … about everything, so I was attracted to the power he was offering, power I thought would make me greater than Lysette. About ten years ago … for ***fun***," she said bitterly, "Léon massacred an entire kingdom."

Christopher's face darkened as he searched his memory. "Floveena," he said quietly. "I remember hearing stories. The knight I was squired to was on a campaign near there and the peasants, who normally have a superstitious explanation for everything, were at a loss for any real explanation as to what happened."

"When I saw the devastation … the innocent children … I knew Lysette was right … again. I left Léon and asked Lysette how I could make up for the last fifty years. She told me I'd have to do a lot of good to make up for all that evil. She sent me to King Lionel and told me to offer him my services as a magical advisor."

"She ***sent*** you to King Lionel? That sneaky…! She knew! She knew what was going to happen to us!"

Aurora laughed bitterly. "You're just now figuring that out? Of course she knew. She was just hoping I would make the right decision instead of the one I did make. She wanted me to just leave when the battle broke out … but she knew I wouldn't."

"That woman has been making me feel guilty for six years about getting you into this mess, and she knew all along what your decision would be?! Unbelievable!" Aurora simply shrugged at him as he gathered his thoughts. "Floveena?" he said again, hardly able to believe everything he had just heard.

"Now do you understand why I didn't tell you? I figured you wouldn't trust me if you knew what I'd done … and we're between a rock and a hard place if you don't trust me."

"Fifty years?" A small smile crept across his lips. "You're older than I thought you were. You're closer to … 250."

She let out a relieved laugh. "Not even close. You're not mad?"

"Mad, no. I'm a little disappointed that this is the first I have heard of all this. We have been friends for years; ex-lovers are normally a topic that comes up in that time, especially if they are holding a grudge." She laughed again. "And I'm a little frustrated that I wasn't given some warning about this guy. But no … I'm not mad."

"I'm sorry. I thought about telling you when I saw his signature in the magic surrounding Gwenyth's mirror prison, but then she made me so mad … and Lysette dropped hints so I thought about telling you, but then she made me so mad … and then Varuk…"

"I know. Every time you wanted to tell me, someone made you mad and then you didn't want to talk about it. Do me a favor: next time, whatever it is, just tell me. I'm not a big fan of surprises."

She smiled. "That was pretty much my big secret, so I don't think you have to worry about any more surprises."

"Good," he said, stepping forward to help her up. "Interesting new look," he said, playfully tugging on one of the black streaks in her blood red hair.

She sighed. "I don't think they will ever go back either. I touched something dark last night … something I didn't think was still inside me." She couldn't look him in the face, and she tried to push herself to her feet without his help.

He used his right hand to tilt her face up to look him in the eye. "We've all done things we aren't proud of. I'm not going anywhere." Then as an afterthought, "Except to breakfast. I think we have kept our hosts waiting long enough. How do you feel about breakfast?"

She let a small smile cross her lips. "I'm starved." He pulled her to her feet and placed her right arm across his shoulders and wrapped his left arm around her waist, easily helping her to walk across the room. His sword bumped into a chair as they passed. "Wearing your sword to breakfast? Isn't that a little paranoid?"

He grinned at her. "With you around, I have to be ready for anything."

She pursed her lips in annoyance. "Very funny."

chapter XVII
a knight's tale

The three travelers descended the stairs to meet their hosts: Christopher supporting Aurora and the pup right on their heels. The royal family was already seated around the smaller, informal dining table when a servant walked in ahead of them to announce them. "Sir Christopher of Calidore and the sorceress, Aurora of Beldain … and their wolf cub."

As the travelers entered the room, the prince leapt up from his seat to offer his assistance to Aurora. The king smiled broadly as he got to his feet, crossed the room and shook Christopher's hand warmly. "Welcome to the kingdom of Maystaire. The tales of your heroic deeds have traveled far and wide. I sent my son and many other messengers to seek you out because I wish to hear your tale." He paused. "All of it."

Christopher seated himself on Aurora's left and the pup immediately jumped into his lap. The king's daughter, a princess of no more than seventeen years, watched Christopher's movements closely, as though she was scrutinizing his every move.

The king continued. "Please, eat your fill. Regain your strength. Anything you have need of will be provided for you as long as you are our guests."

Aurora smiled weakly and began to eat, daintily at first and then more heartily as her strength began to return. Christopher relaxed when he saw that she was feeling well enough to eat and began to look to his own needs. He reached for a piece of bread using his left hand and the princess finally spoke. "I thought people who used their left hand more than their right were servants of the devil. If the stories about you are true, how can you serve God and the devil?"

Christopher simply stared at her, eyes wide and mouth agape, left hand held poised four inches from his mouth, still holding the piece of bread. Aurora cleared her throat to break the awkward silence. "Actually, that's a common misconception that will plague mankind until the twenty-first century."

The princess looked at her, her expression displaying her disdain. "And what of you? You can see the future but you have done nothing to change your own fate? How useless!"

"Aryanna!" the king scolded. "They are our guests! Mind your tongue!"

The princess rolled her eyes and turned her nose in the air just a little more. She stood up from the table and walked away, her long curly brown hair bouncing behind her as she crossed to a harp in the corner and began playing.

Christopher's eyes tracked her every movement as she crossed the room before he finally placed the bread in his mouth.

"She's a little scary," the cub whispered and Aurora struggled to hide her amusement.

Christopher swallowed his bread and followed it up with wine to wash it down. "It's been a very long time since I have felt like an outcast, my every move under scrutiny," he whispered. They continued to eat while their hosts talked, with Aurora slipping little bits of breakfast to the wolf cub under the edge of the table. The princess played several lilting tunes on the harp until they were ready to relocate to the library.

The couches in the library were lavish and cozy. The king immediately lounged comfortably across the largest, with the prince perched on the edge, anxiously awaiting their tale. The princess daintily settled onto another, while Christopher helped Aurora to sit on a third. She was already able to get around by herself, but she had trouble sitting or standing up on her own.

After she was settled, Christopher turned to their hosts. "Where would you like me to begin our tale? My birth? ***Her*** birth?" Aurora glared at him. "Our meeting?"

"How did you meet each other?" the prince prompted.

Christopher smiled. "Very well. We met seven years ago in Sartain, at the court of great King Lionel. A dragon had flown off with his daughter and he had promised the world to anyone who could bring her back. Every knight in the kingdom had tried and failed, all having been defeated by the rogue dragon and some losing their lives in the process."

"Rogue dragon?" the princess interrupted.

Aurora smiled condescendingly. "Dragons are normally hatched and raised by dragon masters, a race of people over the mountains to the south. Only when humans steal young dragons do they become the vicious creatures of legend. Some of these dragons are taught to obey a rider while others kill their captors and must fend for themselves, becoming rogues."

Christopher continued. "I was almost of age, but I was only a squire. After watching the knight I served come back defeated, I suspected that it would take more than brawn to defeat the creature. I tried to encourage my master and to help him plan another attempt, but he was dejected. Soon, there was talk of abandoning all rescue attempts because so many knights had already failed. Fearing for the safety of the princess, I set off on my own to see if I could lend her aid or bring her hope.

"When I reached the dragon's lair, I discovered that instead of taking over an existing natural cave, he had dug his own cave into the earth and built the entrance using rocks from the surrounding area. Upon closer examination, I surmised that removing two specific rocks would bring the whole thing crashing down, blocking the cave's entrance for good. I snuck in and found the dragon sleeping and the princess cowering and crying in a corner. The dragon's tail was blocking her escape, but it kept twitching in its sleep. The princess was afraid she would be flattened by the tail, but it gave me an idea. I managed to find an irregular shaped rock by the cave's entrance and lug it inside. The next time the tail twitched, I slid the rock into place and it created a tiny hole under the tail that the princess could crawl through. I led the princess to the mouth of the cave and loosened one of the rocks for her. The dragon awoke and I could feel the heat of his breath traveling up the tunnel. The princess and I worked together to dislodge the two vital rocks at the same time, bringing the whole thing crashing down on the creature's head just as he was about to reach us. His dying breath was a burst of flame that nearly roasted me alive as I scrambled out of the way. The princess then fainted dead away so I was forced to carry her home on foot."

As Christopher finished, Aurora jumped in. "I was King Lionel's advisor, and he was overjoyed when Chris walked into the audience chamber carrying his beloved daughter. He offered

Chris anything he wanted in return for his heroic deed, but all he wanted was to be a knight, so the king had him knighted on the spot."

The princess scoffed and began twirling one of her curls around her fingers. Aurora glared at her disapprovingly, but Christopher stared at her as if trying to form an opinion. Aurora continued, "About a year after that, a very evil and powerful warlock set upon the kingdom with an invincible army. The army overwhelmed our forces and swept through them as if they were a wheat field. I enchanted Chris' sword, so he was the only one able to kill the invaders, and then I used all the magic I could muster to protect the two of us, making us impervious to harm. Unfortunately, the spell was so large that it drained me and I collapsed from exhaustion."

Christopher took over the narration. "The warlock was infuriated that we had escaped his wrath. We were the only survivors from King Lionel's forces; I had killed some of the warlock's army and injured the warlock himself. Once we were captured and brought before him, he used a powerful dark magic to peer into our souls and see how we had come to still be standing in his way that day. He saw my long list of good deeds, the largest of which was the princess' rescue, and he decided that as punishment he would place a curse on me that I was to help others, never living life for myself until my dying day, or until the curse is lifted."

"I was still unconscious, but my magic was too drained to have been able to protect me anyway, so he was able to see right through me. He saw my friendship with Chris and what I was willing to do to protect him, so he bound us together in the curse, with me protecting his life until the end of my days."

"Or until the curse is lifted," Christopher finished for her when she paused indefinitely.

The princess cleared her throat. "I hate to interrupt again, but why would a being whose whole existence was evil put a curse on you to do good deeds. It makes no sense. You curse a bad person to do good deeds, not a good person. Why?"

Christopher shrugged. "We actually don't know why he chose the punishment he did. We've never seen him again to ask him."

"Please continue, Sir Christopher," the prince said kindly, trying to make up for his sister's disdain.

"So, straight from the battle, with me in full armor, we set out on the first part of a journey that has been going on for six years now. As soon as Aurora was awake, the magic began to draw us in the proper direction to help someone. At first, Aurora resisted the pull, trying to find the strength to regenerate her magic, but the pull became more insistent and painful the more she tried to ignore it."

"That was just the first example of how we learned the hard way about the restrictions of the curse. Any time we ignore a call or I try to use magic to complete a quest for Chris … I get a nice magical jolt to remind me I'm not along to make things easier for him, just safer."

"And so we wander. We have saved maidens from griffins, dragons, wizards, … and mothers," he added with a smile. "We have saved kingdoms from ogres, war, famine and incompetent rulers. We have saved families and their farms, magical creatures of every kind…"

"And we defeated my nemesis," Aurora said softly, and everyone in the room realized that that battle had almost claimed her life the night before. She stood, needing only Christopher's hand to steady her as she did so, and walked to the far corner of the room, her arms wrapped around her upper body as if she was cold.

The princess watched her movements with sympathy while Christopher continued speaking. "Unfortunately, my armor that was a gift from King Lionel when I was knighted was left behind in our haste to leave the scene of our last battle. I'm not even sure what the dark lord did with it once it was taken from me."

The king smiled. "Well, if you are able to stay, I can have a new suit made for you by the palace blacksmith."

Christopher sighed slightly. "I thank you for the offer, but we probably won't be staying long."

"Only until our wounds heal," Aurora added from the corner.

"Yes, and it appears you have had an opportunity to speed that along," the king smiled again.

"Oh, for goodness sake, Father! You don't truly believe this nonsense do you?" the princess scoffed.

"Aryanna!" the king scolded. "How can you disrespect our guests in that manner?"

"Such tales! It is nothing more than a fabrication!"

"And what exactly about our story is it that you don't believe?" Aurora asked coolly, her hair streaked with burgundy and the remnants of black. "The magic?" a feral grin spread across her face.

"Oh please. Every child born knows there is magic in the world and that there are those who can manipulate it. I have no trouble believing that you are one of those people."

"Arya!" her brother hissed, trying to silence his opinionated younger sister. "Forgive her. When our mother passed, she lost her ability to simply believe."

"Please do not make excuses for me. I simply do not understand the fuss being made over a story that is nothing more that a beautiful sentiment with a few dangerous adventures."

"I think it is a marvelous story," the prince interrupted. "The life you lead, the adventures you have, the danger … if I were you, I wouldn't trade it for anything."

"Guille, it is obvious they made it up. None of these things ever actually happen. Curses? Dragons? Dragons do not exist. Some half-awake peasant saw a bird in the distance once and their imagination took over from there. You cannot fight a figment." She folded her arms across her chest.

"I'm sure you'd feel differently if they happened to you," Aurora muttered.

The prince stood up and grabbed his sister by the arm. "Arya! A word?!"

He attempted to drag her from the room but she jerked her arm free. "That is quite alright. I was just leaving anyway, as this conversation bores me. Since their wounds are almost healed, when you boys tire of their farfetched tales, do send them on their way. I am retiring until lunch is served. By your leave, Father?"

The king waved her away in annoyance and turned to face Sir Christopher. "Pray forgive my daughter. She suffers from an inability to believe in things she cannot see, whereas my son has an overabundance. The loss of my queen affected her deeply."

Aurora gazed out the door the princess had just walked through. "Can't believe in what she can't see? A dragon should come carry her off. Maybe then she'd believe us."

Before she finished speaking, the sky turned dark and clouds began to billow, filling the sky. Aurora's face became thoughtful and then worried as she slowly looked down at the talisman around her neck. It was glowing bright green.

A roar was heard echoing through the corridors of the castle, followed closely by a shrill scream and a wave of heat.

"Aryanna!" the king cried, jumping to his feet and rushing from the room with the prince and several servants on his heels. Christopher was about to follow when he glanced over at Aurora and watched her collapse into a chair. He skidded to a halt and waited for an explanation. "What's wrong?"

"Oops," she whispered, glancing up at him with a guilty look on her face.

He glared at her because her hand was clutching the talisman. "What did you do?" his voice was filled with calm anger.

"I was a little mad and kinda muttered that a dragon should come carry her off so she'd believe your stories. And the talisman is glowing..." she said, moving her hand to show him and let him put the pieces together.

"Aurora!" he exclaimed, his shoulders dropping in frustration. "That's a ***big*** oops!" He started shaking his head, scrunched up his face, rubbed his hands up and down over his face a couple of times and then looked at her again. "Go," he said, the calm anger resonating throughout the room as he pointed toward the entrance to the castle. "You stay," he said to the wolf cub as he began to walk out after her in the direction of the stables. He placed his hand on the hilt of his sword at his waist as they set off to rescue yet another damsel in distress. "And she wonders why I'm paranoid," he muttered.

Chapter XVIII
Searching for Dragons

"I'm sorry! I didn't mean to!"

"I swear, you say that one more time…!"

"It's not like I did it on purpose!" she protested. She was riding behind Christopher on Jonathan as they sped through the forest trying to keep the dark shadow in sight.

"Just give me your word that you will destroy that thing as soon as we get out of this mess!"

"I promise," she muttered dejectedly.

Aryanna's screams were echoing through the forest, so even when they lost sight of the dragon, they still had some idea which direction to proceed.

"So now what?" she asked, holding on tight as Jonathan tore through the forest at breakneck speed.

"Are you joking?! I'm making this up as I go! I haven't even got the slightest idea what we're dealing with!" he protested. "I don't suppose you have something useful to add … like what kind of dragon you summoned?!"

"I told you: it wasn't intentional! How should I know what kind of dragon carried her off?!"

Christopher growled out of frustration. "I swear…" He left his thought unfinished, knowing full well she'd heard the unspoken part anyway.

The princess screamed again, drawing them back to the task at hand. They had moved out of the lush forests surrounding Maystaire and were now galloping through the nearby barren mountainous region. The hoof beats of the other knights from Maystaire had dropped off, easily outdistanced by the longer, more urgent strides of their powerful warhorse.

Aurora turned her head from side to side. "I can't hear her anymore."

Christopher pulled back on the reins and halted their forward progress. "Well that can't be good. Can you tell where they went?"

She shook her head and bit her lip. "I can't get a fix on her. My magic is still too drained."

Christopher glanced around. "Can you fly? If you're not too drained, maybe you can see where they went."

She looked at him meekly. "All I get is a few feathers." When he looked at her quizzically to see if she was going to explain her cryptic remark, she lifted her arm to show him where she had sporadically begun sprouting feathers.

"Okay, so you can't shape-shift. What does that leave us?"

Aurora glanced around again. "Do you hear that?" she asked, her eyes searching the hills to their right.

"I don't hear anything. Could it be our dragon?"

"It's definitely something," she said, lost in thought. "Let's check it out."

The travelers turned in that direction, quite unsure of what they would find when they reached the opposite side of the ridge. At the steepest part, both Christopher and Aurora dismounted, continuing up on foot, leaving Jonathan to wait nervously until they returned.

"Right about now, I wish we had an army," Christopher

muttered when they got their first glimpse of what was making all that noise on the other side of the ridge.

Aurora gasped quietly as her eyes took in the sight before them. They had stumbled upon a mining operation. Two rogue dragons and their riders were overseeing about one hundred peasants who were being forced to mine, cart, separate or purify the metal ore from the side of the mountain. Two other dragons, much younger than the ones bearing riders, were chained at the mouth of a large cave like guards at a vault. And then they saw him: the large black dragon they had been chasing with a huge rider in black armor holding the unconscious princess aloft like a human sacrifice.

"Oops," Aurora whispered, realizing how much trouble her loose tongue had gotten them into this time.

"I'm really beginning to hate that word," he said through clenched teeth. "I wish I had my armor," he muttered while drawing his sword.

"Be thankful you don't. It would be very hard to sneak up on anybody wearing it. So what's the plan? Stage a peasant revolt?"

Christopher glared at her. "We don't have enough weapons … and we can't offer the peasants anything other than their freedom to incite riot, which isn't always enough to risk life and limb."

She looked thoughtful for a moment and then glanced out at the five dragons. "If we could get them to turn on their masters…"

Christopher turned to her hopefully. "Do you have anything that could do that?"

She shrugged. "Let me check." She took a moment to check

all the pouches on her belt. "I still have some powder from that unicorn's horn. A unicorn is a delicacy for dragons. It might be enough to stir up trouble so that you can sneak her out."

Christopher thought about it and glanced out across the mining establishment. "You'd better make me fire-proof ... if you can."

"Stone skin too?" she asked, reaching for her belt pouch.

"I believe in this instance that prudence is our friend," he said, waiting for her to work some magic.

She took a pinch of powder from a pouch on her belt and sprinkled it over his head. She whispered "*ne reine*" in Gaelic and then waved her hand to cast the other spell. "You're all set, Hero." She glanced over at the dragons. "Just let me know when and I'll release the unicorn powder on the wind. That should send them into a frenzy."

"Look where he's taking her," Christopher hissed, sheathing his sword and pointing past her. The largest dragon's rider had dismounted and was carrying the princess into the vault cave. The two dragons guarding the entrance shrieked as he passed but made no other move. "We had better do this now. I sure hope it distracts those dragons."

"It will get their attention ... but there's no guarantee they will ignore you because of it."

"And there's no guarantee that your magic is replenished enough to work."

Aurora opened her mouth but found she had no retort. She let out a deep sigh instead. "No matter what happens, I won't let you die."

"That's comforting, especially since you're staying here. And don't argue! You don't have enough magic to protect both of us. Wish me luck … and I will signal you when I'm ready." With that, he scrambled off along the ridge to find a better place from which to descend upon the vault.

"Stubborn fool!" she hissed as she watched him go. "Always has to be the hero!"

He scrambled around the area until he was downwind of the dragons and in the perfect spot where he could drop down and run behind them through the mouth of the cave. *Now*, he thought and watched as Aurora appeared over the opposite ridge and blew a fine powder out of the palm of her hand onto the passing breeze.

"Show time," she whispered, waiting to see what happened.

The results were almost immediate. The largest black dragon reared up on its hind limbs and let out an earsplitting roar. This noise was soon mimicked by the two smaller dragons, who reared up and threw their riders. Finally, the two smallest added their voices to the cacophony, straining against their chains. Christopher chose that moment to drop down behind them and try to sneak into the cave. The first had strained so hard against his chain that it had broken, and he had started running across the clearing. The second, however, had heard some of the rocks Christopher dislodged as he climbed down, and had turned just as the hero reached the ground in front of the mouth of the cave. The dragon roared, opened his mouth and lunged, intending to bite Christopher in half.

Aurora clasped both hands over her mouth in an attempt not to shriek as she watched the dragon bite down on Christopher's midsection. He hadn't actually been damaged, but the dragon appeared to be chewing on him, with

Christopher's legs sticking out of its mouth like a pair of tooth picks. The other four dragons were in a frenzy, tearing each other apart in order to be the first one to get up in the air and spot the unicorn.

Christopher was kicking his legs in an attempt to get some leverage, but it wasn't working. He could feel the heat of the dragon's breath and the vice-like grip of its teeth around his waist, but he couldn't seem to do anything about either. Every time the dragon tried to bite down, the sound of teeth grinding rocks echoed in his ears. The dragon's forked tongue flopped, smacking him right in the face and giving him an idea. He managed to pry his dagger loose from his belt and plunged it straight through the tongue, pinning it to the soft flesh beneath. The dragon let out a howl of pain and spit him across the cavern's entrance with a burst of flame, clawing at its own tongue in panic. Christopher bounced off the far wall and then managed to scramble beyond the dragon's reach and down the entrance of the cave. When he got the chance to examine himself, he found his clothes and hair were singed, but the rest of him was intact. *So much for your magic being at full strength*, he thought before disappearing down the tunnel.

Christopher descended into darkness, and he quickly found himself wishing he had a torch to light his way. He was creeping along with one hand out to feel the wall and the other extended out in front of him. After tripping over his third rock in as many steps, he wondered aloud, "Why do I always leave her behind just when I need her the most?"

He felt a small, warm furry creature scurry up the outside of his pant leg and alight on his right shoulder. "Because you're stubborn and you insist on doing everything the hard way," her voice said in his right ear. "I thought someone who can see in the dark might be useful."

He patted her little ferret body. "I love it when you read my mind." She nipped his finger playfully and coiled her body around his neck.

They continued into the bowels of the earth, breaking the silence only when Aurora warned him of an obstacle. Each was secretly hoping the other had a brilliant plan for when they caught up with the black knight, who *was* in full armor.

The darkness soon began to dissipate, and they realized they were almost to the vault. They came to the mouth of a cavern and as he peered around the corner, Christopher was amazed at what they had stumbled upon.

"They must work the metal somewhere else and store the finished products here," she whispered, turning her head as she stared at the fully-equipped armory. "You wanted weapons."

He glared at her. "That was not what I meant and you know it!" he hissed. "I didn't want the weapons in the hands of our enemies!"

The black knight had laid the unconscious princess on a bare display table and had removed his helmet that looked like a giant pair of dragon wings.

"Stay here," Christopher commanded as he plucked her from his shoulder and set her on the ground before he drew his sword. He stepped into the cavern and bellowed, "Unhand the princess!"

Aurora, who had transformed back into human form, pinched the bridge of her nose between her right thumb and middle finger and closed her eyes. "Oh brother!" However, her eyes flew open and her body tensed up when she felt the cold steel of a knife blade against her throat.

The black knight, still with his back turned to the hero, began to laugh, a deep rumbling laugh. "Sir Christopher, still doing good deeds selflessly, I see."

Christopher inhaled sharply as he recognized the voice. "Barbas," he growled as the knight turned to face him.

The black knight tilted his head mockingly at Christopher. "I thought knights usually wore armor. Did you need to borrow some?" he asked, waving his hand to indicate all the armor around them.

"Thank you, no, I will fight you without it."

The black knight looked thoughtful. "And where is that pretty sorceress that always seems to get you into trouble instead of keeping you out of it?" He looked past Christopher to the mouth of the cavern and grinned happily. "Ahh, right on cue."

Christopher risked a glance behind him and saw Aurora, in human form, but her hair black with anger, being held with a knife to her throat by one of the other dragon riders from outside. "You okay?" he asked.

He's going to die a horrible and painful death, Aurora thought.

"Okay then," Christopher muttered, turning back to his foe. "If you will not release the princess then we have to fight for her."

The black knight's eyebrows went up in amusement. "You, without your armor or your sorceress to protect you, want to fight me?" He laughed again. "If you truly wish to die today, then step forward."

"Unable to help your knight, eh?" the other dragon rider

wheezed in her ear, his breath an affront to her senses. "How can you hope to help him if you are powerless to help yourself?"

Aurora's eyes turned black to match her hair with electricity crackling across their surface, the talisman glowing a steady green. "If you actually think I'm powerless, then you're in for quite a ***shock***," she hissed as electricity rippled out from the talisman, used her body as a conductor, and began coursing throughout his body. He lost control of his limbs and dropped his knife, giving Aurora the chance to turn around and shape-shift into jaguar form in one smooth motion, leaping at her attacker with feral vengeance.

Christopher and Barbas were fighting heavily, the sword fight swiftly moving from one end of the cavern to the other. "Sounds like your sorceress has her hands full with my lieutenant," Barbas laughed, listening to but not seeing the commotion on the other end of the cave.

Christopher grinned confidently. "Actually, I'm quite sure it's the other way around." Their swords clashed again as Christopher forced the bigger knight back a few steps. "By the way, I never got the chance to thank your master for this wonderful way of life he's given me."

"I will have to tell him when I deliver these weapons." Their swords clashed again, this time Christopher being forced back several steps.

"How is his face, by the way? Did that scar ever heal?"

The larger knight brought his sword down in a sweeping arc, intending to cleave Christopher's head in two. "He is actually still mad about that. I cannot imagine why."

"His overconfidence was his undoing there," Aurora purred, circling the fighters. "So good to see you again, Barbas."

"Ah, come to give your knight the unfair advantage again, I see." The larger knight was beginning to get winded, swinging his sword with less vigor.

"I wouldn't dream of it. Actually, I thought I'd keep the fight fair," she purred as she prowled around the outskirts of the fight, watching intently.

Nice to see your magic's back, Christopher thought as he once more went on the offensive.

It's not. I just finally figured out how to tap into the talisman without emotion.

Another dragon rider rushed into the cavern and Aurora turned to deal with him, swishing her tail happily. Christopher tripped over a rock and stumbled backward, giving an advantage to the larger knight. He wound up for the killing blow … then suddenly crumpled like a rag doll in a heap on the ground, right on top of Sir Christopher.

"What the…!" he exclaimed, pushing the big knight off and looking up in alarm.

"I thought you might need some help," the princess said with a smile, cradling the mace she had used to knock out the black knight on her left shoulder while offering her right hand to help him up.

chapter XIX
the future dawns

Christopher's jaw fell open as he accepted the helping hand. "You didn't faint?" he asked, dusting himself off.

She laughed. "Goodness, no. I got tired of screaming so I pretended to faint. What took you so long?!"

Christopher threw his arms out in frustration. "Excuse me?!"

"Do not mistake me, I knew you were coming and I *am* glad to see you, but I honestly expected you sooner."

"You did see what I had to get past outside, didn't you?"

"You are cute when you are frustrated," she said with a smile as she slipped her arm through his.

Aurora prowled back into the cavern licking her lips in satisfaction. "That was fun." She glanced back and forth between Christopher and the princess. "And what have you two been up to?"

Christopher gave her a pleading look, begging for help, but Aurora pretended not to notice. "Are all your adventures this much fun, or am I just lucky?" the princess asked with a grin.

Aurora tried not to laugh as she eyed the unconscious knight and the mace on Aryanna's shoulder. "You knocked out Barbas?"

"Oh, do you know him? But yes, and I would have done it sooner but you have no idea how hard it was to find something I could lift that was heavy enough to give his skull a good crack."

Aurora laughed, "Well, he does have a thick skull." When neither of the humans responded, she shook her head. "Nevermind. It appears our lovely warlock friend wasn't content to just rule Lionel's kingdom. He looks like he's equipping another army."

"The warlock who cursed you?" Aryanna asked wide-eyed.

"Yes. That buffoon you knocked out is his right hand." Aurora prowled around the cave. "You might want to replace your knife."

Christopher looked up in surprise. "Wait, how did you...?" Then he shook his head. "Nevermind. I really should know better than to ask." He selected one from the stash and slid it into his belt sheath angled at the back of his waist. "Now what?"

Aurora gave him a feral grin and transformed back into human form. "You and the princess get all the peasants out of here. We'll meet back at Jonathan."

"What are you going to do?" Christopher asked, taking Aryanna by the hand, the other still clutching his sword. "On second thought, I don't want to know."

Christopher and the princess had to gingerly feel their way to get out of the tunnel. When they finally reached the light of day, they were shocked to find the clearing completely deserted. The carcass of the young dragon who had tried to eat Christopher was blocking the entrance to the cavern, so the gallant knight gently lifted the princess over the creature's spine-covered neck.

"What happened to him?" she asked quietly.

A look of pain crossed Christopher's face as he let go of

Aryanna's waist and cautiously approached the creature. "The other dragons attacked him, and since he was still chained, he couldn't really defend himself. His masters..." His face hardened as he turned to Aryanna. "We need to check the mine," he said gruffly, "and make sure all the workers are out."

Absentmindedly, Christopher grasped her hand and headed for the mouth of the mine, causing her to smile shyly to herself at this protective gesture. The mine was deserted, leading Christopher to believe that the rampaging dragons had done far more than simply serve as a distraction. They had scared the peasants into a revolt and had frightened the soldiers into desertion.

After making sure that the mine was indeed void of life, Christopher began to climb the ridge with a heavy heart, still leading Aryanna by the hand. He turned his sad gaze on the dragon when they reached the crest of the ridge, and she could tell he was upset. "What troubles you?" she asked.

"He died needlessly. Dragons are very majestic creatures. In the hands of the right master, they are nothing to be feared. But these..."

Aryanna brushed one of his curls off his forehead and he jumped at the sudden contact. She laughed. "I shall not hurt you." She tilted her head at him thoughtfully. "Guille frequently told me stories about the knight that providence forgot, and I always imagined him as hard and rather evil. I was angry because my illusions were shattered. You were not supposed to be so good. It was childish of me, but you were nothing like what I expected ... and you are unlike anyone I have ever known." She turned her big brown eyes on his and he felt his vocal chords seize up in fear. "So noble..."

she moved closer, "and kind..." and closer, "and heroic..." As she was about to kiss him, a huge explosion ripped through the clearing, completely obliterating the mine, the vault, and all traces they had ever existed. Christopher and Aryanna were both knocked off their feet by the blast and Jonathan reared up in fear.

The dust began to settle and they looked up to see Aurora walking out of the smoke, untouched by the destruction that surrounded her. "I'd love to see the warlock supply his army now."

Christopher glared at her. "A little excessive?"

She pouted as she looked around. "I happen to be quite proud of the way I contained the blast." She then narrowed her eyes at Aryanna briefly. "I think I'll meet you back at the castle," she said hastily. "Enjoy your ride." And with that, she vanished in a puff of smoke.

Aryanna dusted herself off. "Is she always like that?"

He sighed. "Pretty much. You would think I would be used to it by now."

The other knights from Maystaire finally began to arrive, drawn by the noise of the explosion. They were overjoyed that their princess was safe and that Sir Christopher had once again managed to save the day. They all rushed off at a gallop to alert the king and the prince that she was safe. Jonathan however, who had just rushed to the rescue, was in no hurry to get back, and no amount of coaxing or kicking could change his mind.

"I'm sorry about this," Christopher said sheepishly as they plodded along through the forest. "He's not usually this stubborn."

Aryanna laughed. "The rest of today rushed by so quickly,

it is nice to allow my thoughts to catch up." She turned her big brown eyes on his again. "I am sorry for my behavior at breakfast. I just … thought you were making it all up to get attention from people like my father."

"That's silly. If I were going to make it all up, I would do it to get the attention of someone like you." Her eyes danced with delight as he turned beet red. "I really just said that, didn't I? I have been spending too much time with Aurora."

She smiled and wrapped her arms around his neck. "I knew I liked you," she whispered as she drew him closer and kissed him. As soon as her soft, full lips touched his, all of the fight went out of him and he couldn't do anything but hold her.

Aurora arrived back in her room at the castle and reluctantly slipped the talisman from around her neck. She gazed thoughtfully at the soft green glow that was emanating from it and lovingly ran her fingertips over the jewel's surface. "It seems a shame to destroy it," she said quietly.

"Then don't," the wolf cub said, lifting his head. He had been sleeping on the rug in front of her fire until that moment. "Just because it used to belong to someone bad, doesn't mean it shouldn't be allowed to do some good."

Aurora smiled and set the talisman down on the night table. "You're not just talking about the talisman. You're talking about yourself."

The cub had jumped up on the bed beside her and he sheepishly placed his head in her lap. "I just…"

She laughed. "We're not planning to leave you behind. We just didn't want you along today because we were afraid you would get hurt. And with my magic a little on the fritz, I wouldn't have been able to protect you. But, you're a valiant little hero, and we would be proud to have you as a traveling companion."

"Valiant? Sir Christopher called me that, too. What does it mean?"

"It means courageous or having courage. Why?"

"Well, you've both used it to describe me and since I still don't have a name, I thought maybe..."

Aurora smiled. "I like it. Valiant. It suits you."

The pup tilted his head proudly. "I can't wait to tell Sir Christopher! Is he in his room?" He jumped off the bed in his excitement.

"Uh, no, actually. He's not back yet."

The cub looked at her in confusion. "Why are you back so soon? Where's everyone else?"

"They're coming. Besides, three's a crowd."

"Huh?"

She sighed. "Nevermind."

Christopher and Aryanna arrived some time later, and the royal family was overjoyed at her safe return. Her brother affectionately chastised her for her skepticism that morning and the king gushed over the speed with which Christopher and Aurora were able to deliver his daughter back safely to him.

Christopher pulled Aurora aside while the royals were conducting their reunion. "Where's the talisman?" he whispered, the glowing green stone conspicuous by its absence.

"It's gone."

"You destroyed it?" he asked, surprise plain in his voice.

"It's gone," she reconfirmed.

He smiled. "You don't need it, you know."

"I know. It was just nice having the power boost every once

in a while." She caught Aryanna smiling at Christopher coyly. "So ... how was the ride back?" her tone insinuating something.

He glared at her. "There aren't enough words to describe how annoyed I am with you for that."

She tried and failed to hide a grin. "Sorry. I just thought it might be good for you."

"Cruel is more like it. Showing me what I can't have until the curse is lifted."

She laughed outright. "Who says you can't have it? Bring her with. Personally, I think this one would be more fun than Gwenyth. And more useful. Did you see her with the mace?!"

"Ohh! Hush!" he hissed in annoyance as the royal family turned their attention on the heroes.

"Sir Christopher! Aurora! Anything you wish, you have but to ask and it shall be yours. Any reward could not be as great as the service you have done for me this day!" the king cried, approaching them with arms outstretched.

Christopher bowed deeply. "I thank Your Majesty for your generous offer, but we want no reward. All we ask is your hospitality for one more night, and then we must be on our way. The magic is calling."

When Aurora didn't add her confirmation to his statement, he jabbed his elbow into her ribs. "Ow! ... oh, yes, the magic is calling." She looked at him in confusion, but no one else caught the look.

The king and the prince looked disappointed, but the princess looked utterly crushed. The king then smiled hospitably. "Of course you may stay another night. I would much prefer to keep you indefinitely, but it appears that your quest has not forgotten you ... even if the rest of the world seems to. Please, enjoy the castle tonight. In the morning, we will have a proper send off for you."

Christopher bowed again and then he and Aurora left the room at a hurried pace. They had nearly walked to the other side of the palace before Aurora broke the silence. "There's no one following us. Care to tell me what that was about?"

"She kissed me!" he blurted out. He came to a dead stop, threw his head back in frustration and stared at the ceiling.

"Yeah, and…?" she asked, waiting for the rest of his explanation. When he didn't answer, she simply stood there, watching his face in silence.

"I can't do this! We have a calling; I can't afford to get distracted."

A huge grin broke out on her face. "You're being ridiculous. Just admit you like her."

"I will do no such thing. I just think we should get out of here before she gets too attached."

Aurora tried not to laugh. "***She***?" When he glared at her, she threw up her hands in defense. "Alright. But in that case we should probably sneak away tonight. I just hope Valiant is ready to travel."

"Who?" he asked in confusion.

"The wolf. He chose a name: Valiant."

Christopher smiled. "Quite appropriate. You sure we can sneak away tonight?" he asked changing the subject back again.

She groaned. "One-track mind. Yes, if you want to, we can sneak away tonight." She glanced around. "It's an awfully nice castle. You sure you want to leave?"

"Impossible woman!" he growled as he stomped away

down the hall to prepare for their journey, her laughter following after.

In the dead of the night, they snuck out of the castle under cover of darkness. As always, they let the magic guide them as they struck out for parts unknown. Christopher was riding Jonathan, while Aurora and the pup ran alongside; Aurora was in jaguar form so that she could keep them both within hearing distance. The magic was pulling, guiding them to their next adventure and those in need of help. By mid-morning, they had left Maystaire and Princess Aryanna far behind. They traveled along in silence, for even Valiant had nothing to say.

Finally, Aurora could stand it no longer. "Alright, explain to me why we snuck away in the middle of the night like criminals."

"Sir Christopher is afraid of the princess," Valiant commented, bounding along beside her.

Aurora tried to hide her grin, but her feline teeth gleamed in the sun. "Our hero … afraid … of a woman? I can't believe such a preposterous accusation."

Christopher sighed deeply in annoyance. "If you two don't stop you will find me traveling fifty paces behind you for the rest of the journey. I cannot stop you from ridiculing me, but I refuse to listen to it."

"Then just admit that you're scared because you like her."

"I will do no such thing! I am not afraid of Arya. I was just sparing her the heartache of attachment and separation that would have plagued her if we had left this morning."

"Arya? She's 'Arya' now?" Aurora laughed. "Okay, if you aren't afraid of her, how *do* you feel about her?"

He sighed. "I'm not in love with her, if that's what you're

getting at." He regarded her carefully, searching for the right words. "She was beautiful, and intelligent, and she has an adventurous spirit..."

Aurora smirked and whispered to Valiant, "He can tell all that after one day?"

"...but she was unwilling to take me at my word, and she doubted all of our adventures until she experienced them herself. If she feels that way about dragons, I can only imagine how she feels about God. Besides, she decided I was worth her time only after I had proved my stories true. That's not real love."

"No ... real love is devotion, self-sacrifice, loyalty and friendship. It shows patience and kindness, not skepticism and disbelief. It's not rude ... and it's not based on deeds. It's wanting to scream how you feel from the mountaintops because you want the entire cosmos to know, like life is empty or incomplete without the other person. It's knowing what the other person needs almost before they do ... putting their needs before your own. It's living life for someone other than yourself. Without those things, love can't exist."

Christopher looked at her in surprise. "You told me you never loved Léon, so who are you talking about? Some other mysterious stranger who is going to pop up?"

"What, can't a girl have any secrets?" she asked, a twinkle in her eye. When he raised his eyebrows at her, she thought about what she had said. "I mean ... that ***won't*** try to kill us."

He gave her another annoyed look and then glanced around. They were traveling over the mountains to the northwest of Maystaire, and the terrain had started to get harder for Aurora and Valiant to handle. Out of necessity, Aurora took to the skies in hawk form and Valiant got to ride on Christopher's lap. Night began to close in on them and they found themselves hard pressed to find a sheltered place to spend the night.

Aurora soared low right next to Christopher. "Well, I have good news and bad news. Which would you like first?"

He sighed. "What's the bad news?"

"I think it's going to snow."

He sighed again. "And the good news?"

"I found a cavern of sorts where we can spend the night. It's not much, but it will keep the snow off our heads."

Christopher nodded and allowed her to lead the way. The cave she had found was actually too small for anyone to be comfortable in, but they made do. Aurora set up one of their many blankets as a sort of tent to extend the cave so that Jonathan could have shelter and Christopher set up the fire in the back of the cave. By the time Aurora had unpacked some of the animal skins from the saddle bags, a thin layer of snow had already accumulated on the ground. "It's going to be a cold night," she commented, laying out one of the skins for Valiant and Christopher to curl up on.

"We knew these days were coming," he laughed, rubbing his hands together by the flames to warm them up. "They always do."

"Someday, I'm going to live somewhere warm … with no snow."

Christopher raised his eyebrows. "No snow? Where's the fun in that? How else would you mark the changing seasons?"

"Hallmark decorations," she said with a shrug. When he simply stared at her, she shook her head in frustration. "It spoils my fun when my pop culture references are lost on you."

He smirked. "Let me guess: you want me to laugh even if I don't get the joke."

"Especially if you don't get the joke."

He seemed to think about that for a moment. "I'm going to use a phrase you once said to me: 'Nope, sorry, ain't gonna happen.' Did I get that right?"

She laughed and collapsed into a heap on another skin. "I forgive you for always missing the joke. Hearing you say ***that*** made it all worth it. Go ahead and get some rest; I'll keep watch."

"Don't you still need to recharge?"

"I can keep watch!" Valiant piped up.

Aurora smiled. "I'll be alright. Besides, I have a lot I need to think about."

Christopher looked at her in concern, but consented to laying his head down on the skin and curling up, falling asleep almost immediately. Aurora morphed into jaguar form and curled up, staring out at the swirling snow, and Valiant crept up beside her. "If you ever need someone to talk to, I'm here. And I promise not to tell Sir Christopher."

Aurora smiled and nuzzled the pup's head with her cheek. "Get some rest. I'll wake you when it's time."

Aurora stayed up, lost in thought, watching the swirling snow and allowing visions of the future to wash over her. Some visions made her cry, others made her laugh, and still some made her want to scream in pain or panic. When the time came to wake the others, she felt completely refreshed by her visions and was ready to take on the world.

She pounced on Christopher playfully. "Time to get up!"

"Oof!" he gasped as the wind was knocked out of him. "What the…!" he flailed his arms trying to fend her off.

Valiant awoke and decided to join in the fun, leaping on Aurora's back and biting her ear playfully.

"Okay! Everybody off!" Christopher groaned, giving Aurora a good shove and sending them both rolling across the cave to crash into Jonathan's flank. The big horse turned and nipped Valiant's tail, bringing all the wrestling to a halt with the pup's yelp of pain.

"Spoilsport!" Aurora growled, morphing into human form.

Christopher rubbed his shoulder where her large paw had landed on him. "Nice to see the snow has put you in a better mood this morning. And you look rested … even though I ***know*** you didn't sleep."

"Good visions," she replied, putting her hands together over her head and arching her back to stretch her lower vertebrae. She pulled a heavier, fur-lined tunic out of one of the saddle bags. "Put that on. I don't think we're going to get a break in the weather until we reach the other side of the mountains."

Christopher pulled his tunic off over his head and then looked up in alarm. "Wait! Where will that put us?" He tossed the shirt he had just removed to her and pulled the warmer one over his head, throwing his unruly hair into even more disarray.

She looked thoughtful as she put the tunic away, as if listening to the magic for the answer. Then she laughed. "You're not going to like this."

He sighed. "That's what I was afraid of. You're taking me home, aren't you?"

Aurora looked sheepish. "It's not me!"

"Let's just hope they're happy to see me." He had finished picking up the rest of the furs and putting them away by this time. "Ready to brave the cold?" He scooped Valiant up under his arm before climbing into the saddle.

Aurora had just finished tucking their makeshift tent away when she looked up at him. She blinked her yellow feline eyes at him as the rest of her morphed to match. "Just follow the black cat." Her teeth gleamed as she turned to lead them through the snow.

They traveled for three more days through the mountains, the weather slowing their progress considerably. Aurora spent most of the trip in cat form, the black of her fur a beacon amidst a sea of white snow. By the fifth day, they finally started to descend from the snowy mountains. Aurora got her first glimpse of the town where Christopher had grown up as the valley stretched out below them. They reached the town of Calidore with little incident and Christopher looked around in disbelief.

"It has been ten years since I have been home … but nothing has changed. Everything still looks the same."

Aurora laughed, now in human form behind him on the horse so as to avoid startling the peasants. "You may soon find appearances are deceiving." She smiled at her companion in triumph, having believed for some time that he truly was a farm boy under all his armor and knightly ways.

Even though he had not seen the town in ten years, Christopher was able to navigate the streets with relative ease. The farm where he had grown up was on the outskirts, and as they approached, they could hear the familiar sound of wood being chopped around the back of the main house. The thatched roof had a layer of snow on it, and there were two very young children playing barefoot in the snow with a pair of dogs near the front stoop. The older child looked up as they approached.

"Mama! Mama!" he cried in alarm, rushing into the house with little sister and dogs in tow.

"Hullo!" Christopher called out.

A young woman appeared in the doorway with an infant in her arms. She examined Christopher with a shocked but aloof air. "Airn!" she called to the back of the house. "We have visitors!"

A man appeared from around the back carrying an armful of cut wood. Jonathan reared up in surprise, but the travelers were able to keep their seats despite their own shock. Except for the short beard and the build of a farmer, Christopher felt as if he were staring at his own reflection.

Aurora had to suppress a laugh. The dark curls, the penetrating eyes and the pout of disapproval were unmistakably the same as Christopher's.

"Airn?" he asked in disbelief, managing to gracefully dismount without unseating Valiant or Aurora. The dogs barked in confusion.

"Christopher?" the other said, dropping the wood in disbelief. Even their voices were uncannily similar. "You are still alive?"

Christopher sighed. "Don't sound so disappointed," he said with a laugh as they embraced. The woman in the doorway looked on, almost sadly, before turning back into the house.

"Where have you been?" Airn demanded.

"All over. You wouldn't believe most of the stories if I told you."

"I have no time for stories. I have a farm to run ... something you would know nothing about."

Christopher looked surprised. "***You*** have to run? Where's Father?"

Airn looked at his older brother gravely. "Father went to the Lord … soon after you were knighted." Aurora noticed a bitter tone in the last part of his statement.

Christopher regarded his brother sadly. "Little brother, I'm sorry to have forced you to bear the burden alone."

"Thankfully, I was not entirely alone. I had Creada, who is now my wife, to help with the burden that should have been yours as first born. And do not look so shocked. Naturally we hear all sorts of stories out here, so of course we knew you'd been knighted. We hear all kinds of other things, too," he added, the last bit said with his eyes fixed on Aurora's stoic face.

Christopher shook his head, the pain apparent in his eyes. "I would gladly have taken the burden from you if I were able. Unfortunately, life didn't allow me that luxury."

"Of course not. Being Father's favorite, you were allowed to become the carpenter's apprentice rather than staying at home to learn the farming trade. Then, fortune smiled on you again and you became the favorite knight of the king. Spare me the sob story that you feel is your charmed life. Take your wife and return to your precious king."

Before Christopher could answer, Aurora's voice rang out, cutting through the air like a knife. "Do I look like a wife?!"

Airn raised his eyebrows in disapproval. "Not really, no. Who are you then?"

"My name is Aurora, and I have the ***honor*** of traveling with your brother. That is all."

Airn stared at her in disbelief. "Aurora? Of Beldain? From

the stories?" He turned to his brother in shock. "Are the stories true?"

The conversation between the brothers continued, but Aurora was no longer listening. The snow before her seemed to be swirling and a vision began forming of two people on horses coming down the path from the mountains. The rider in the lead was dressed in peasant garb, long dark hair braided back and under a scarf and a hood. The rider on the second horse looked as if he had tried to dress as a peasant but had opted for a warmer royal outer cloak. As the vision came into focus, she could even hear what they were saying.

"Guille, I am glad you came along, but if you do not hurry we will never catch them."

"Arya, this is ridiculous. There are hundreds of other men you could have. Why do you have to go chasing after the one with a noble quest who does not want you?"

She laughed and spurred her horse faster. "He does want me. He just does not know it yet. If we can just catch them, I will prove it."

"Aurora!" Christopher's voice rang out, cutting through the vision and drawing her back to reality. "What did you see?"

Aurora sighed and shook her head. "The love of your life. And she's on her way here."

Christopher looked at her in confusion. "Wait … you don't mean…?"

"Yep. Afraid so. And she's almost to the town."

"That's not funny."

"That's why I'm not joking. My suspicion is that when we weren't there in the morning, she and her brother set out to find us."

Christopher's head snapped around so he could look her in the eye. "Oh great! Now what?"

"Fight or flee, Hero."

"Those options really don't work for this situation and you know it."

Aurora jumped down from Jonathan's back with the pup in her arms. She smacked the horse on the rump and sent him in the direction of the barn. "Then we hide." She turned to Airn who had been standing there, staring at them in disbelief. "Do you mind if we come inside? Just until a little problem goes away."

The poor man glanced back and fourth between his brother and the sorceress, still trying to fathom the fact that his brother didn't lead the charmed life he had always thought, but he agreed and led them inside.

"Why does everyone think we're married?" Christopher growled under his breath as they entered the house.

"Well, I ***am*** a ball and chain of sorts," she laughed.

"What?"

"Nevermind."

Chapter XX
Persistence Pays Off

"I need a drink," Airn said, crossing to the hearth and pulling down a jug. He raised his eyebrows at his brother and offered him a mug, which Christopher gladly accepted. "And the lady?" he asked, offering her a mug as well.

"What I really need is a martini." When Airn just stared at her, she smiled, "Ale would be great."

Airn yanked the cork on the jug with his teeth and filled the three mugs.

"A word of advice," Christopher said as he accepted the mug, "if you don't understand what she says, it's easier to ignore it. The explanation is just as confusing."

Airn drained his mug and stared at her incredulously. "The stories cannot be true!" He filled his mug again.

Christopher wheezed as the strong brew slid down his gullet. "Is this Dad's recipe?"

"Yes," he replied, "with a few of my improvements."

Christopher's eyes began watering as he took another swig.

Aurora glanced from one brother to the other before she drained her mug in one swallow. When she held it out for Airn to refill, his jaw fell open. "The stories ***are*** true … well, most of them anyway," she conceded.

"There are no such things as dragons, ogres and whatever else, and you certainly do not battle them!"

Creada entered the room with a squalling infant in her arms. "Airn! Lower your voice, you are upsetting the children!"

Aurora gave up the argument, letting Christopher take over, and took great interest in her full second glass of ale. The swirling liquid seemed to catch the light, and she saw Aryanna and her brother along the main road of Calidore. "Excuse me, but have you seen a large chestnut warhorse pass by, either carrying a man with dark curly hair, or the man with a red-haired woman?" Aryanna was asking.

"Aye, there was something about the woman. Powerful. Strange hair. Black streaks. They were headed for Airn's farm, on the outskirts of town."

Drat, Aurora thought. *I would have attracted less attention as the cat.*

"This is Calidore?" the prince muttered in disbelief. "Imagine, such a noble knight could come from such humble beginnings," her brother commented. They persuaded their horses to travel just a little bit faster. "What are we going to do when we find them?"

Aryanna smiled. "Convince them to let us join them in their quest." When her brother stared at her in disbelief, she laughed. "What, you thought I was going to bat my big brown eyes at him and get him to give up his quest to come home and marry me? Where would the fun be in that? You are not the only one in this family who craves adventure."

Aurora laughed to herself and took a small gulp of ale. *I like her. In spite of everything, I like her.* She slowly came back to the conversation around her.

"Airn, darling, we have never left this valley. Maybe there are a great many things in the outside world that we have never encountered," his wife was saying, the infant finally sleeping in her arms.

"I know it's hard to believe. We had trouble believing it at first."

Speak for yourself, Hero, she snapped through their unspoken bond. He glared back over his shoulder at her.

"They simply do not exist!" Airn protested.

"Maybe if one attacked your peaceful little village you'd believe they exist," she muttered bitterly. As soon as she realized what she had said, she gasped in horror and clasped one hand over her mouth and the other flew to her chest. She visibly sighed in relief when she realized that the talisman wasn't there, but not before she got a reproachful look from Christopher. Her hair rippled orange for a moment in embarrassment.

"I am not going to believe they exist just because you say so and make empty threats."

The dogs outside began barking, and Valiant, who had stayed quiet all this time looked up at Aurora. "Our royal problem just arrived."

"It talks!" Airn yelped in surprise, jumping backward out of his chair.

A determined knock sounded at the door, cutting off Airn's next tirade. Creada glanced around at the strange group already assembled in her cottage and cautiously approached the door, unsure of what new surprise lay in store. She pulled open the heavy oak door, and found Aryanna standing on the step, her cloak hood thrown back, a simple scarf in her hair, and wearing servant's clothes. Nothing but her bearing betrayed her station; however her brother was quite a sight in his random assortment of royal and peasant clothes, betraying his regal stature and his inability to let go of the luxuries that came with it. "May I help you?" Creada asked, eyeing them cautiously.

"We seek Sir Christopher of Calidore and were told he had come here. May we enter?"

Creada stepped aside and Christopher sighed visibly in defeat at the sight of the princess. "What are you doing here?" he asked, setting down his ale, unsure of what to think.

Aryanna smiled at him as she removed her cloak. "Sneaking away without even saying goodbye? That seems awfully cowardly for a hero."

Aurora crossed her arms. "Funny, that's what I said."

Christopher scoffed in annoyance, "You're no help."

Airn glanced from Christopher to Aurora to the newcomers. Then, he reached over and snatched Aurora's ale from the table and drained it in one gulp.

The prince pulled his hood back to reveal he was still wearing a crown. Aurora laughed and Airn's jaw fell open. "A prince? Now there is a prince in my house?"

Aryanna turned to her brother and shook her head in disappointment. "I told you we were traveling in disguise. That meant you were supposed to leave your crown at home."

Aurora smiled. "I think he missed the memo."

Aryanna looked at Aurora quizzically and then turned her brown eyes on Christopher. Part of him truly wanted to flee in terror at the sight of her, but another part was intrigued by this feisty creature who had risked her own life to follow him. "Highness, why are you here?" He backed up a few steps.

"I have come to beseech you to allow us to join you in

your quest." She took several steps forward. "And do not tell me that it is no way for a lady to live because Aurora seems to have managed just fine." Aurora smiled with pride and satisfaction, while the princess took two more steps forward, forcing Christopher to take two more back.

"Aurora! A little help here!" he begged.

"What do you want me to do about it?"

"You're supposed to protect me…!" His back was now against the far wall.

Aurora looked away from the entertaining spectacle the prince presented for inspection and glared at her partner. "Excuse me?! Nowhere in my job description does it say I have to protect you from fawning women! Ain't gonna happen! You're on your own, Hero!"

Aryanna smiled coyly at Christopher as she cornered him against the far wall. "I promise you will never wish for any life but the one I will give you," she whispered as she stood on her tiptoes and kissed him.

"Aryanna!" the prince cried in astonishment.

Christopher grasped Aryanna firmly by the upper arms and pushed her away. "Milady! Will you desist?!"

His words were nearly drowned out by the deafening roar that echoed off the snowy landscape. Every head in the room turned to the shuttered window in shock, wondering what was on the other side.

"Blast it, Woman!" Christopher swore as he crossed to the window to peer out through the crack.

"I didn't do it, I swear!" Aurora protested, coming up behind him and peering over his shoulder in apprehension.

A burst of flame shot past the window and Aurora swore

under her breath. Christopher's eyes went wide as the creature came into view. "What is that?" he asked slowly.

"Turns out that ***would*** be my fault," Aurora said sheepishly as she noticed a healing knife wound in the creature's shoulder. "That's the chimera I wounded in order to get its boiling blood."

"It must be tracking you," Valiant piped up. "Most animals never forget the scent of the one who injured them."

"Great," Christopher muttered. "No wonder the magic's pull wasn't urgent. We were leading it home." He glanced around the room. "And me without my armor."

Aurora gasped and looked him up and down, remembering where they had left it. A grave look came over her face, and she looked him straight in the eye. "I'll get it. Wait for me." And with a flash and a puff of smoke, she was gone.

Aryanna coughed and waved her hand to cause the smoke to dissipate. "Where did she go?"

"To get my armor." Christopher offered no further explanation and continued to peer out the window at the strange creature. It was the largest lion he had ever seen, nearly the size of Jonathan, but instead of a tail, it had the head and neck of a poisonous serpent, and from the arch of its spine was the head and neck of a goat. Each of the three heads spewed flames, and the three different cries sent a shiver down Christopher's spine unlike anything he'd ever felt.

Creada had fled to the back room to hide with her children at the first sight of the creature, and the prince had sat down in a chair and was cowering in the corner, but the rest were still staring through the crack in the shutters.

"How do you plan to proceed?" Aryanna asked.

Christopher looked at her in surprise. "I have no idea. I've never seen anything like it before." The lion head roared and a woman's scream filled their ears. "Blast!" he exclaimed, drawing his sword and heading for the door.

"What are you doing?" Airn hissed in disbelief.

"Without your armor, you will be killed!" Aryanna protested, clutching at his sleeve to stay his hand.

"I can't allow an innocent to die in my stead. Aurora will return in time to protect me, and if not, God will." With that, he pulled open the cottage door and charged the creature.

The chimera sensed his approach and turned, spewing flame across his path and causing the snow to hiss as it turned to steam. "I'm beginning to think this was a bad idea," he muttered as he ducked behind a snow drift. *Aurora! Get back here!* He peered over the drift and could only hope his partner had heard his silent cry.

The chimera had decided to abandon its attack on the passing villager, but it now had him pinned down with no way to advance or retreat. He glanced around, hoping an idea would come to him, when the bucket from the well sailed into view on the end of its rope and hit the goat head from behind. Christopher and the chimera both turned to see where it had come from just in time to see Aryanna reeling the frozen bucket back in with the rope to wind up for another shot.

"Run, Christopher!" she cried, swinging the heavy bucket above her head on the rope and once again sending it flying at the chimera.

Christopher scrambled out from behind the snow drift just as a spurt of flame disintegrated the bucket, causing Aryanna to dive for cover. "Get out of here!" he yelled at her. He dashed through the snow, charging the creature in an attempt to give Aryanna the chance to escape. His plan, however, only worked slightly; the serpent head lashed out at him, venom dripping from its fangs and breathing fire. Christopher dropped to his knees and rolled forward, coming out of his forward motion directly underneath the serpent head. One quick slash of his sword and he had removed that threat, but the boiling blood splashed on his right arm as the entire tail fell past him to the ground. "Argh!" The chimera turned, roaring in pain, and knocked him off his feet with a swipe of its claws. It pounced and landed on top of him, pinning his shoulders in the snow and sending his sword flying. Its claws dug into his left shoulder as Christopher struggled to get out from beneath it, and it brought its large lion's head down level with Christopher's face and growled, drool dripping onto his face.

"It's times like this I hate my life," Christopher grumbled, trying desperately to wriggle out from underneath the monster. "I could really use some HELP!"

Aryanna let out an earsplitting scream just as Christopher's right hand closed around a trowel buried in the snow. The chimera turned, distracted by her scream, lifting its weight off of Christopher's right shoulder just enough that the knight could swing the trowel upward to stab the creature in the gut. The chimera's two remaining heads cried out in pain and anger before its body began to convulse. The boiling blood was dripping down the trowel onto Christopher's hand and arm, but he was fighting through his own pain to inflict further damage on the creature. Suddenly, the creature's cries became more frantic and pained.

"What the...!" Christopher exclaimed, throwing his free hand up to protect his face as the creature collapsed on top of him.

"Christopher!" Aryanna screamed as the valiant hero disappeared under the massive carcass of the chimera. She rushed to his side and attempted to dig through the snow to free him, but the animal was too large and she couldn't seem to make any progress. "Someone help me!" she yelled back to the house, knowing Airn was still watching from the window. "Guille, please!"

At that moment, with a flash of lightning, Aurora appeared with a pile of armor at her feet. She quickly glanced around until her eyes settled on the princess, practically in tears, kneeling next to the chimera and digging in the snow.

"Please help me!" the princess cried again, not even noticing that the sorceress had appeared and was now standing behind her.

Aurora's eyes took on a faraway look as she began chanting in Gaelic, invoking the magic once again, this time to dispose of the chimera before Christopher suffocated. A wind rose, the snow began swirling and Aryanna sat back in disbelief, wiping away her tears and staring up in amazement as the carcass began lifting off the ground. As soon as the body was high enough, Aryanna grasped Christopher by both wrists and pulled him to safety. The carcass became engulfed in the swirling snow until it seemed to compact into a ball that began shrinking until it vanished completely.

Aurora knelt down next to Christopher and began examining his wounds. He was lying in the snow with his head in Aryanna's lap, his left shoulder and upper chest slashed, the blood flowing freely. His right hand and arm were burned, the skin starting to blister. "What hurts more?" Aurora asked.

Christopher breathed in slowly, hissing in pain. "My arm." He lifted his right arm so she could see the full extent of his burns.

Aryanna tore a piece of cloth from her tunic and pressed it into his bleeding shoulder. "Just lie still," she said gently.

"Argh!" he growled, clenching his teeth. Then he looked up at Aryanna's concerned face. "Why did you do that?" he asked, his tone caring and disbelieving.

"Which part?" she asked with a small smile.

"Ugh, I'm going to be sick," Aurora muttered under her breath, but the other two didn't hear her.

He groaned as he tried to sit up but both women pushed him back down. "You risked your life to save me. Why did you do that?"

The left corner of her mouth went up slightly in a smile. "Because I have never met anyone like you before … and I am in love with you."

He looked at her in surprise. "But why? How can you be?" He shook his head. "I'm nobody. Look at where I come from!"

"Dense," Aurora muttered, fiddling with the pouches on her belt.

Aryanna smiled and his heart skipped a beat. "You think I care about that? You constantly give of yourself with no thought of reward. You risked your life to save mine and you did not even know me. I have never met anyone who would do that for me … not even my father. And just now, you were willing to give your life to save these villagers. You are almost too good to be true … as if I made you up…" She had leaned down, her nose only inches from his.

Aurora smeared salve on his burned arm and watched the two of them out of the corner of her eye. "I'll be right back," she said, standing up and walking into the house, knowing full well that neither of them was listening to her. Once she had crossed the threshold, she turned to look at each of the brothers. "You two were a lot of help, I see."

Guillaume stood up and straightened his tunic. "He is incredibly brave. I admit that I am not."

Airn growled, "He is not brave, he is crazy!"

Aurora laughed. "Do you still feel envious?"

He scoffed. "No."

Outside in the snow, Christopher and Aryanna were still simply staring at each other. "You have yet to tell me how you feel."

Christopher swallowed as he stared into her deep brown eyes. "A knight never betrays his feelings. He is chivalrous … he doesn't let feelings get in the way of duty…" Her eyes became sad and she started chewing on her lower lip in disappointment, so he raised his hurt left hand to the back of her neck. "Oh … hang duty!" With that, he pulled her to him, content to let the rest of the world fade away as he kissed her.

Aryanna moved her right hand, inadvertently putting extra pressure on the wound in his shoulder, and he pulled away from her, crying out in pain. Aurora rushed from the house to his side, bringing with her a wet cloth to wrap around his salve-covered burns. She quickly finished with the burns and then proceeded to move Aryanna's hand and the piece of cloth she'd used to try to stop the bleeding. Aurora ripped open his shirt to completely expose the wound, sprinkled some purple powder on it, rubbed her hands together and pressed them into Christopher's mangled flesh. He groaned in pain and squeezed the princess' hand tightly in his left. Aurora's hands began to glow brightly, and within moments, the blood had ceased to flow between her fingers. Finally, when she pulled her hands away, there were four new scars running across his shoulder and chest where the wounds had been.

"There. Good as new … sort of," Aurora said, getting to her feet and offering a hand to help him up.

"Thank you … as always." He turned to the house and noticed that Airn had opened the shutters and was watching them with a look of shock on his face, while the prince had ventured onto the stoop looking very much like a frightened child.

"***That*** was following us?! Arya! You neglected to mention that we were in danger!"

The princess scoffed. "We were traveling without an escort or protection. There was always a chance we were in danger. Honestly!"

"Still believe we're making things up, Little Brother?" Christopher asked, testing the range of motion on his newly repaired shoulder.

"I take it back," Airn said, running his right hand through his unruly hair in exasperation, the same way Aurora had often seen Christopher do it. "I believe you. You can keep your life, be it charmed or cursed. I am perfectly content to be a farmer."

Christopher laughed. "I'm happy for you and your good fortune. Treasure the life you have here."

Airn came down the front step and embraced him. "Good journey. May God keep you safe."

"And may God keep you safe, Little Brother."

Chapter XXI
Facing the Future

Christopher and Aurora stood in the barn, preparing Jonathan for another journey.

"We can't take them with us. We have to take them home."

Christopher pulled his torn tunic off over his head. "What about the magic? Won't you be in pain if we ignore the call?"

Aurora laughed. "Believe it or not, I can't feel the magic pulling at all. I suspect we're meant to take them home."

Valiant pounced on a rat in the corner of the barn. "The prince would just slow us down if we took him with us. And he lacks his sister's courage." Jonathan snorted his agreement.

Aurora shook her head. "You know it's bad when even the animals notice he's cowardly."

Christopher pulled on a new tunic and then pulled on a fur-lined cloak. "Then I guess we'd better get moving." Aurora grinned and morphed into cat form.

The heroes exited the barn and found the royals, both astride their horses, ready to start the long journey through the snow. "Well, that answers that question," Aurora grinned, her feline teeth gleaming.

Airn, watching from his doorway, felt his mouth fall open. "I need another drink," he muttered, turning his back on the mystical and finding comfort in his simple life.

"Everyone ready to travel?" Aurora asked, stretching before taking her place at the head of the caravan.

"Certainly," Aryanna replied, pulling her hood tighter to keep out the wind. "Where are we bound?"

"To Maystaire, Milady," Christopher said, following Aurora to the head of the caravan.

"But why? Surely there are other people in need of help?! More adventures to be had?!" the princess protested.

Christopher looked at her, a thin smile on his lips. "Aurora assures me that for now, we are only needed as an escort back to Maystaire. Besides, I do not believe that our life is quite what your brother expected. He looks as if he is ready to return to the palace."

"Besides, I suspect your father has no idea where you two have run off to," Aurora said with a grin.

The prince looked guilty, but Aryanna simply looked annoyed that Aurora had figured them out. "Shall we?" Christopher asked, hoping to break the tension.

"We need to get moving before nightfall or we're going to be stuck here … and I don't really think your brother is ready to offer us that kind of hospitality." Christopher nodded, and the caravan started off through the town, heading back to the mountains and eventually Maystaire.

The trip back was fairly uneventful, with Aryanna occasionally casting betrayed looks in Christopher's direction and the flustered hero doing his best to focus on the task at hand. By the third day, there was a biting chill in the air, and it had nothing to do with the weather. Aurora did her best to keep out of everyone's way. Luckily, the weather was with them and they were able to reach Maystaire before nightfall on the fourth day.

The king was relieved to see his children returned unharmed, so he willingly put up the heroes for another night. Aurora curled up in cat form on the rug in front of her fire, but Christopher paced the halls of the castle, his feelings and the resulting dilemma running through his mind. He knew that Aryanna wanted to be with him and that she would willingly join them in their quest, but he didn't truly feel that that was the life she deserved. He wanted her to be happy, but as much as she made him want to believe it, he didn't feel she could be happy with their life. He could promise to come back for her once the curse was broken, but he didn't want her to have to wait that long. He found himself strolling through the castle gardens in the pale moonlight, wishing there was someone to talk to about everything.

"Wish granted," Aurora purred from the shadows.

He looked up in surprise and found her glowing yellow eyes staring back at him. "I did not realize you were still awake."

"It's kind of hard to sleep with your thoughts screaming through my head like that."

"I'm sorry, I just..." he sat down in exasperation and put his head in his hands, his elbows resting on his knees. "I don't know what to think."

Aurora laughed and lay down at his feet. He pulled his left hand away from his face and began scratching her behind the ears. She gave him an annoyed look but allowed the show of affection to continue, knowing full well it was helping to calm him. "Trust your feelings. Your whole life you've followed your heart and done the right thing. Has that ever steered you wrong?"

"No ... it just got us cursed."

Aurora shook her head. "It got ***you*** cursed. ***I*** got in this mess all on my own, thank you very much. And I don't necessarily see this as a bad thing. So, I guess the real question is: do you love her?" Christopher didn't answer, and Aurora swished her tail. "Who am I kidding? Of course you do. You've been in love with her since you rescued her. So what's the problem?"

Christopher flicked her ear in annoyance. "Sometimes I do not consider it a blessing that you can read my thoughts."

"This would not be one of those times. And you are avoiding my question."

He sighed. "The problem, believe it or not, is that I ***am*** in love with her. I want her to be happy. And I don't believe she would be happy with our life."

"Don't you at least want to give her the chance to decide that for herself? Maybe she'll just be happy to be with you."

He glared at her in disbelief. "I don't wish to subject her to the life we lead."

"That's still something ***she*** should decide. My vote: bring her along. She's more fun than Gwenyth, she's more helpful in a fight … and she seems to want to come."

He stood up. "You make it sound so simple, but it's not."

"It could be."

He walked away, and turned to look back at her. "Maybe things will look different in the morning."

Aurora got up from her crouched position. "They often do."

The two heroes went to their rooms and proceeded to sleep for the remainder of the night, Aurora and Valiant curled up by the fire and Christopher in his bed in the next room.

The next morning, the heroes came down for breakfast to find Aryanna and the king in a heated discussion. The king looked incredibly angry, and there was a look of wild defiance on the princess' face. "Father, you are being unreasonable!"

"I am ***not*** being unreasonable! My unmarried daughter wants to go gallivanting across the countryside with this knight! It is quite improper for a lady!"

"What does that make me?" Aurora muttered under her breath, but no one heard her.

"I will not be dissuaded! I love him and he loves me!"

"You have no idea of his feelings!"

"I know he loves me, though his chivalrous nature will not allow him to admit it! I cannot ask him to give up his quest, so I will join him … and you cannot stop me!"

The king inhaled sharply, as if preparing to unload another tirade on his daughter when Aurora audibly cleared her throat, drawing attention to their arrival. "Ah, Sir Christopher, Aurora, I trust you slept well?"

Aurora smiled sweetly. "Of course. It's hard not to sleep well thanks to your hospitality. I trust we're not interrupting," she said with a grin, knowing full-well they were.

Aryanna laughed. "Of course not. My father and I were just ***calmly*** discussing the options for my future."

Christopher coughed, quite embarrassed that he was an integral point of the discussion. "Your Majesty, we thank you for your hospitality but it's time we were on our way."

"I'm coming with you," Aryanna announced.

Christopher rolled his eyes and looked to Aurora for reinforcements. She was, however, simply trying not to laugh.

The argument began all over again, continuing until the king bellowed, "I forbid you to go! An unmarried princess having adventures! It is preposterous!"

"What about a married one?" Aurora asked with a smirk.

Christopher turned to her in shock. *What are you doing?!*

Making up your mind for you. Your reward: ask for her hand. He shook his head at her vehemently. *You know you want to,* she scolded.

Christopher took a deep breath, his eyes betraying fear. "Your Majesty, the life I lead is not an easy one. It takes an extraordinary woman to survive in my world." He smiled at Aurora. "However, your daughter has shown herself to be quite extraordinary, and I have come to care very deeply for her. As I do not know when my travels will bring me back here again, I feel it is unfair to ask her to wait for me. However, with Your Majesty's permission, as a reward for rescuing Arya…" he took a deep breath to build his courage, "I wish to take her hand in marriage … if she will have me."

Aryanna's face lit up and she turned to her father with pleading eyes, begging that he say yes. The king sighed. "If this is what you want, Daughter, then I will not deny this noble knight the right to choose his reward." Aryanna nodded, speechless for once at the way the day's events had come about. "Then I will consent. I will begin preparations for a royal wedding at once. We will need at least a fortnight to get ready, so please, make yourselves comfortable in the palace until then." He walked away muttering to himself about everything that needed to be taken care of.

"Are you sure this is a good idea?" Christopher asked, as Aryanna slipped her arm through his.

Aurora smiled. "I can see the future, remember? Everything turns out the way it's supposed to."

Christopher smiled and then hugged her. She didn't move,

simply standing there perplexed until he released her. Aryanna was trying desperately not to laugh at the uncomfortable look on the sorceress' face. "Everything we have been through together," he said, "all the times you have been there when I needed you, all the times you have saved my life…"

"What are friends for?"

He looked her full in the face. "I want you there with me … with us. If I'm going to do this, if I'm really getting married, then I need you by my side … like always."

Aurora took a deep breath and then smiled a thin smile. "I wouldn't miss your wedding for anything."

"Christopher, please go find out what my father has planned. We need a little girl time."

He glanced from one woman to the other. "Oh, that can't be good." However, he bowed gracefully, "Ladies, by your leave," and did what he was told.

As soon as they were alone, Aryanna turned to the sorceress. "Are you alright?"

Aurora laughed. "Princess, you are far too observant. No, I am not alright. I lied to him when I said the magic wasn't pulling."

"Is there anything I can do?"

Aurora sighed. "Unfortunately, as long as we ignore the call, the worse I'll feel. I'm just worried that I'll ruin the wedding." She glanced at the princess. "He wants me with him, but I can't control the shocks. I want to see you both get married, but he won't be happy if he's worrying about me. We can give in to the call as soon as you're married, but until then…"

"We have a tower room. No one ever uses it. You could hide there until after the wedding. It even has a window overlooking the pavilion where we are going to have the ceremony so that you can be there in spirit."

Aurora smiled at the princess' generosity. "Thank you. That will work quite well."

That night, under cover of darkness, Aryanna took her to the highest tower in the castle to hide out until after the wedding.

Chapter XXII
Happily Ever After?

The day of the wedding was drawing nearer and Christopher found himself becoming more anxious with each passing day. Not only was he soon to be married to a princess, but his best friend was missing and no one seemed to know where she was. His unease was beginning to affect everyone, even his betrothed.

"Tell me again how you and Aurora met," Aryanna pleaded, hoping to distract him from Aurora's prolonged absence.

He smiled. "Arya, you have heard the story at least half a dozen times."

"I know, but you have yet to give me some clue as to how the curse gets broken."

He laughed. "That's because I don't know. Only Aurora knows that. The warlock's instructions were simply that I would die if she told me how the curse was lifted before it happened."

Aryanna looked at him in shock. "You mean she carries that secret alone? ***And*** she must deal with the consequences if you break the rules of the curse? I cannot imagine how hard that must be. I know that I would have been tempted to tell you if the responsibility belonged to me."

"Aurora has no regard for her own life, but she would never do anything to endanger mine."

Aryanna laughed as they strolled through the castle halls. "I do believe she is in love with you."

He looked at her, thoroughly perplexed. "You jest. I have never seen anything all these years to give me that idea. How did you decide that?"

"The little things. Someday, I shall prove I am right."

The day of the wedding arrived and there was still no sign of Aurora. While Aryanna and Valiant had both assured the hero that she was around, he had seen no sign of her and he was really beginning to worry. "This isn't like her. I have spent everyday with her for six years, and I haven't seen her in almost a month. Something doesn't feel right."

"I saw her yesterday," Valiant tried to reassure him as he dressed for the wedding. "It's a big castle; I'm not surprised you haven't run into her. She told you she wouldn't miss this. Has she ever let you down before?"

Christopher finished combing his hair and turned to the pup. "No, she always finds some way to come through for me." He straightened his new red velvet tunic and the black fur cloak. "How do I look?"

"Very regal. The princess will be quite impressed. And Aurora will be proud."

Christopher took a moment to compose himself and then he squared his shoulders and took a deep breath. "It's time."

The people began to congregate in the pavilion and Aurora looked down on them from the tower window, the brightly colored costumes contrasting sharply with the blanket of white snow covering everything. She *was* proud when she saw Christopher appear in his red and black outfit, and her heart ached that she couldn't be by his side as she had promised. She only hoped that

Christopher would forgive her after the fact. She turned away from the window and sat at a small writing desk, holding the quill to a half finished letter. The door to her tower room creaked open, and Aurora looked up to see Valiant sneaking into the room.

"Why aren't you watching the wedding?" she asked in a scolding manner.

"Thought you could use the company. He's worried about you, you know. He can't even hear the echo of your thoughts anymore."

She nodded. "I know. I'm shielding the connection because I don't want him to feel my pain. But it will be over soon enough. He'll be married and everything will work itself out."

She had stood up, but then she doubled over in pain as the electricity arced across her body. "The ... bottle..." she strained, attempting to point to the bedside table.

The pup jumped onto the bed and grasped the small clay bottle in his teeth, hurrying back to Aurora's side. She struggled with the cork and was finally able to get a few drops on her tongue. The shocks subsided immediately, but it was several minutes before she was able to stand up.

"They're getting worse," Valiant commented, sitting back on his haunches and watching her in concern.

"They'll be over soon." She crossed to the window and looked down again on the pavilion. Aryanna looked stunning in a white fur trimmed dress and cloak, her hair twisted back up away from her face and the curls cascading down, intertwined with brightly colored ribbons. Although she couldn't hear the words, she could tell where the friar was in the ceremony. "We've made the right choice," she said, going back to the desk to finish the composition. Once she had finished, she curled up on the bed and tried to get some rest, Valiant tucked into the curve of her body.

In the pavilion below, Christopher was standing facing his beloved, both her hands grasped in his, a ribbon wrapped around their wrists to bind them together. The friar gave them permission to seal their union with a kiss, and as their lips met, Christopher felt that this moment was his happiest. That feeling, however, was short-lived. As soon as they shared their first married kiss and then turned to the people gathered, Christopher doubled over, his entire head exploding with pain and his body feeling as if it had been trampled by a horse.

"Christopher!" Aryanna exclaimed. "What is it? What has happened?"

He groaned. "It's Aurora. Something's wrong." He winced in agony. "She's in so much pain … but I can't tell where she is."

Aryanna sighed in defeat. "She has been hiding in a tower. I will take you to her."

The newlyweds left their bewildered guests under her father's watchful eye and hurried through the castle to the tower. Upon reaching the bottom of the tower stairs, they could hear Valiant's mournful howl coming from above. Christopher raced up the steps, intending to come to the rescue once again, but quite unsure of what he would find. He flung open the door to the tower, his entry unbarred, and the sight that met his eyes was one he would carry with him for the rest of his days. Aurora was curled up in the fetal position on the bed, her cheeks wet with tears and her features frozen in a cry of pain, and there was a strange burn mark on her bosom. Christopher rushed to her side and gripped her right hand in his right, brushing her hair out of her face with his left. As he did so, her hair seemed to shimmer and it slowly changed to a golden blonde, even the black streaks. "Aurora, can you hear me?" he asked softly, searching for some sign of life. Valiant continued to sit on the bed beside her and howl in sorrow.

"Christopher," Aryanna said, bringing his attention to the writing desk by the window. "She has written you a letter."

Christopher stood and came up beside his wife. He peered down at the letter written in Aurora's ornate handwriting and was shocked by what she had written.

Chris,

By the time you read this, you will be married ... and I shall be gone. It is now time for you to know what the warlock told me on that fateful day so long ago. "Doomed to protect him until your death, your love has made you a slave. When he finds love and is loved in return, on his wedding day will you draw your last breath." I apologize for not keeping my promise to stand by your side at the wedding, but I figured my absence would be more forgivable than my death in front of your guests. Please don't mourn for me, as keeping you safe has been the only thing that has ever made me happy ... and today is the happiest I've ever been. The curse is broken, but please don't ever stop being ruled by your kind heart. It will never steer you wrong ... never. You are free, my friend, but I shall always be watching you and yours ... from wherever I end up. Congratulations, and here's to "happily ever after."

Aurora

"By all that I have ever held holy!" he exclaimed, turning to look at his wife. "She knew. She knew that our love, that our marriage would bring about her death, and she pushed for us anyway."

Aryanna slid into Christopher's arms and stared at Aurora in admiration. "She stood by and watched while the love of her life pledged his love to another, sealing her fate forever. She has an incredibly steadfast nature; she has done something not one woman in a thousand could do."

Valiant stopped howling and looked over at the couple. "The magic's been pulling at her for weeks, so she was shielding you from her pain, but in the end, the pain was too much for her."

"I have been blind," Christopher whispered. "All along, she knew that I would not return her love and she bore the awful secret of how the curse would be lifted all these years in spite of that."

"Yet she died thinking only of your happiness."

Valiant cocked his head and stared at the sorceress. "Your happiness made her happy. Just look at her hair."

"I never thought I would see it that color." Christopher buried his face in his wife's shoulder for a moment before looking over at his protector once more. "We shall have a funeral for her after sundown. The altar for our wedding shall be her funeral pyre."

"We can just wait here until our guests have retired for the night. Then we can hold a private funeral for her later."

Christopher nodded his consent, simply staring at the lifeless form of his protector.

The sun finally set and Christopher carried Aurora down

to the courtyard. Only two guests from the wedding had remained behind for the funeral, and Christopher was actually quite grateful they were there. As he laid Aurora's lifeless form on the pyre, Gwenyth turned her face into her husband's shoulder in sorrow.

"Oh, Liam, how dreadful!"

Christopher stepped back from the body and looked over at his friends and new family. Aryanna was standing nearby, Valiant in her arms and a handkerchief held to her eyes; the king and Prince Guillaume were standing behind her, both looking very forlorn; Princess Gwenyth and Duke William were wrapped in each other's arms, both teary eyed. Christopher leaned down and kissed Aurora on the forehead. "Goodbye, my guardian angel. May you at last find peace. You did your job well, protecting me right up to the end. I know you will continue to do so from heaven. I owe you my life … and now my happiness as well. Farewell." As he finished speaking, he touched a torch to the pyre and watched as the bright flames began to engulf Aurora.

They all stood in silence and snow began to fall, but the flames seemed to burn more brightly with the change in weather. Christopher stood with his arms wrapped around his wife, holding tightly to her as if his life depended on their bond.

"I never thought she'd give up 349 years of magical existence for ***you***."

Christopher jerked his head around in surprise. "Lysette?"

The sorceress was standing beside him in the swirling snow, seeming to have appeared out of nowhere.

The older sorceress smirked at him. "I figured that when

it came down to it, she'd let you die. I never actually thought she'd do this."

Gwenyth stared at the sorceress. "If you can see the future, why did you not see this?"

Lysette ignored her comment. "I hope your happiness, and your life, are worth it."

"Look!" Aryanna exclaimed, pointing at the night sky. A ribbon of colored lights had begun shimmering in the sky above the pyre, the colors rippling like the colors of Aurora's magical hair.

Christopher smiled at the sign from beyond the grave. "Something tells me she thinks they are."

Lysette merely scoffed in annoyance.

That night, as the newlyweds climbed the stairs to turn in for the night, Christopher was still shaking his head in disbelief. "349? I never would have guessed."

Aryanna laughed. "You keep thinking about what Lysette said, and I keep thinking about something from Aurora's letter."

"And what might that be?"

"What did she mean, 'Here's to happily ever after'?"

Christopher laughed. "Oh, that. We once had a conversation about how 'happily ever after' is a fairy tale ending and Aurora was of the opinion that it can't be achieved by any real person. I felt differently. I guess that was her way of saying that if anyone can do it, you and I can."

Aryanna smiled triumphantly. "Is that so?" She pulled Christopher to her and kissed him. "In that case, 'here's to happily ever after'!"

the end

CPSIA information can be obtained
at www.ICGtesting.com
Printed in the USA
BVOW04s0940200317
478895BV00001B/34/P